THE SECRET OF THE
FIFTH MYSTICON

THE SECRET OF THE
FIFTH MYSTICON

LIZ MARSHAM

NEW YORK

{Imprint}
MAKE YOUR MARK

A part of Macmillan Publishing Group, LLC
175 Fifth Avenue, New York, NY 10010

MYSTICONS: THE SECRET OF THE FIFTH MYSTICON. Mysticons characters, design, and elements © 2018 Nelvana Limited. Mysticons is a trademark of Nelvana Limited. All rights reserved. Printed in the United States of America by LSC Communications, Harrisonburg, Virginia.

Library of Congress Cataloging-in-Publication Data is available.

ISBN 978-1-250-16499-5 (hardcover) / ISBN 978-1-250-16500-8 (ebook)

Our books may be purchased in bulk for promotional, educational, or business use. Please contact your local bookseller or the Macmillan Corporate and Premium Sales Department at (800) 221-7945 ext. 5442 or by e-mail at MacmillanSpecialMarkets@macmillan.com.

Book design by Heather Palisi

Imprint logo designed by Amanda Spielman

First edition, 2018

1 3 5 7 9 10 8 6 4 2

mackids.com

If you thought to steal this tome, beware!
It is protected by spells everywhere!
The Mysticons fight ancient magic.
Defy them, and your end will be tragic.

In a time of darkness and blight,

Mysticons will rise. . . .

THE SECRET OF THE
FIFTH MYSTICON

In Which Mares Are Saved,
Orcs Are Bashed,
a Choice Is Made,
and a Voice Is Heard

1

AS THE MYSTICONS PILED INTO THE STRONGHOLD, TIRED AND elated and all talking at once, the first thing Em noticed was Doug. He and Malvaron, the Mysticons' Astromancer mentor, were sprawled on the couch. Malvaron was watching Doug play *Remembered Realms V: Rite of the Blood Queen* on the Hex-Box. On Malvaron's other side, Choko, Zarya's pet foz, was snoozing peacefully.

"Good shot, man, but you should be using your fire arrows, and aim for the beak," Malvaron was saying. "That's a frost roc, so you get double damage when—"

Breaking off mid-sentence as he heard the four girls come in, he jumped up and whirled toward them. "How was Mare-Con? Tell me everything!" he instructed.

Em saw Doug look over with a mixture of eagerness and regret, and right away she felt a tightness in her chest. "Doug," she said, "I just want to say how much we appreciate you giving up your tickets to the Twinkly Mare convention so we all could get in. We know you were really looking forward to it, and—"

"Oh my goblin," Arkayna cut in. As she hurried over to Malvaron, the Mysticon magic surrounding her faded. Her staff dissolved into thin air, and her green-and-white Dragon Mage outfit transformed into her street clothes, revealing her as Princess Goodfey of Drake City. "You were right, Malvaron. Kymraw was *totally* ready to destroy the whole convention, not to mention hurt thousands of fans, just to get her hands on all two hundred of the limited-release Super-Sparkle Crystal Pegacorns."

Malvaron nodded in satisfaction. "I will never understand why that biker troll loves Twinkly Mares so much, but I knew she wouldn't be able to resist."

"Yeah, and we were ready for her!" Piper chimed in,

jumping up on the table and striking an action pose, her magical golden hoops held high over her head. "And we kicked her—" Suddenly she pulled up short and seemed to deflate. Her Mysticon Striker outfit shifted into her everyday clothes as she lowered her arms and plopped down to a cross-legged position. Even her pointed elf ears seemed to droop. "Well, *first* we had to wait for Kymraw to show up. That part was less fun, 'cause we were supposed to be all *quiet* and *blending in* and *not touching all the toys. . . ."*

"*You* were having less fun?" Zarya snorted. "*You* weren't disguised as the back half of a unicorn!"

"Aw, come on, big Z," said Piper. "You know you and Arkayna were the only ones tall enough for that costume. It's human-size!"

"And I would have taken the back and let you have the head," Arkayna added. "But you *did* say that you didn't care about seeing the convention."

"That is *not* what I *meant!*" Zarya flung her bow to the side, dismissing the magic that made her the Mysticon Ranger. Shoving her hands in the pockets of her newly revealed hoodie, she stomped over to the couch and flopped down between Doug and the still-sleeping Choko. The foz woke up with a squeak of protest. "Whoops, sorry," she said, patting him. "I had a tough day."

Choko climbed onto her shoulder and chittered, wrapping his tail around her neck. He pointed to the screen, and Zarya immediately perked up. "Heeeey, *Remembered Realms*! This is just what I need! Doug, load up my save!"

Doug's single eye blinked in surprise. "Oh, uh . . . sure, Zarya." He handed over the Hex-Box controller. "Here you go. But, uh—"

"Sweet!" Zarya grabbed the controller, Choko jumped up onto her head, and they both leaned forward, immediately immersed.

"As I was *saying*," said Em pointedly, "Doug." The big cyclops looked over at her. "We know how much you wanted to see the convention, and we all—" She looked at Zarya and Choko, deep in concentration on the game, then at Arkayna, relaying the highlights from the battle as Piper acted them out and Malvaron laughed. Em sighed and pressed on, reaching into her belt pouch. "We *all* wanted you to have this." She fished around in the pouch, fingers skating past various magical orbs and dwarven tools. Finally she pulled out a horse figurine with wings and a twisted horn. The colors of its crystalline body seemed to change and shimmer in the light.

Doug's eye got huge. "Is . . . is that . . . ?" He sprung off the couch and bounded over to Em. "Is that Glimmer Gust, the limited-release Super-Sparkle Crystal *Pegacorn*?!?"

Em nodded, letting the pouch fade away with the rest of her Mysticon Knight outfit. She handed the horse toy to Doug, who accepted it reverently.

"Wait!" Piper shouted, freezing in the middle of miming how one of Kymraw's orcs got hopelessly tangled in a convention banner. "We got a Glimmer Gust? That's fabtacular! When did that happen?" She vaulted off the table and ran over to Doug. "Can I see it? Huh?"

"Piper!" scolded Em. "It's a present for Doug, since he had to miss the convention. And I *just* gave it to him."

"Oh! Right." Piper backed off sheepishly. "Sorry, Doug."

Doug smiled down at her. "It's okay. I'm just glad you all had fun and saved the day."

"Did we ever!" chirped Piper over her shoulder, already headed back to finish the story for Malvaron.

"And we couldn't have done it without you," said Em.

Doug shrugged awkwardly. "Aw, you would have figured something out. You always do." He ducked his head, fiddling with the toy in his hands. "You're the heroes, after all."

"No, really!" insisted Em. On impulse, she reached up to put her small dwarven hands over his large ones. "We only stopped Kymraw and her gang because of *you*. You gave us the tickets and described the whole layout of the convention so we knew exactly where to wait. You're a hero, too."

Doug shrugged again, forcing a smile. "Thanks for saying that." He held up the Pegacorn, and his grin became more genuine. "And thanks for this. So much. I'm gonna go find a place of honor for it."

Thoughtfully, Em watched him lumber off toward his room. Then she glanced at her bangle-phone and snapped to attention. "By the Hammer of Harmon, look how late it is!" she said.

"Yeah," chuckled Zarya from the couch. "Time flies when you're bashing orcs."

"You're on night patrol tonight, right, Em?" called Arkayna, her hands raised over her head as she acted out whacking Kymraw with her staff.

"Yeah, I got it." Em concentrated, and the magic washed over her once more. A pink mask appeared on her face, and her clothes transformed into the pink-and-purple armor of the Mysticon Knight. She gestured, and a large sword with a flame-shaped purple blade appeared in her hand. "See you all later."

Zarya gave a half-hearted wave from the couch, then swore as an enemy in the game surprised her. Choko chirped and shook his little paw at the screen, taunting the enemy on Zarya's behalf. Arkayna had reached the end of her tale and was bowing elaborately while Malvaron clapped. None of them seemed to hear Em's farewell. Piper, though, raised her head from her prone position on the floor, where she was playing the part of the freshly defeated Kymraw. "Bye-eeeeee!" she sang out.

A few hours later, Em was still flying over Drake City on her griffin, scanning for trouble. The lights of Magi Mall glowed beneath them, the stars twinkled above them, danger could lurk in any shadow . . . and Em couldn't stop thinking about her conversation with Doug.

"I mean, I know everyone *likes* Doug," she mused to the griffin. "You like him, right, Topaz?"

Topaz squawked noncommittally.

"Well, okay, but you don't *not* like him," continued Em. "You just haven't spent that much time with him. And that's the point! We like him a lot, but we never try to make him a real part of the team. He just ends up hanging out in the Stronghold, helping Malvaron with stuff and making us snacks."

Topaz clacked her beak at the mention of food.

"They're great snacks, don't get me wrong! And I know that we have our Mysticon powers, and Malvaron has his magic, and Doug . . . doesn't have . . . any of those things. But, still! What do you think?" Em took a deep breath of the night air, then shook her head. "Wait, why am I asking you?" She patted the brown feathers on Topaz's flank fondly. "I guess I just know what it's like to feel like you're a sidekick in someone else's adventure. I hate to see him feeling left out."

"OUUUUUUUUT!" cried a girl's voice that seemed to come from the sky. Em startled, almost tumbling off of Topaz's back. The voice echoed and wavered strangely as it came again, louder than before. *"LET ME OUUUUUUUUUUT!"*

In Which Em Is Told Many Old Things
and Jumps to a New Conclusion

2

"GREAT GOBLINS!" YELPED EM. SHE GRABBED FOR TOPAZ'S harness to steady herself, looking around wildly. Topaz craned her head around and stared at her rider.

"Why are you giving me that look?" Em asked.

The griffin snorted.

"Didn't you hear her?"

Topaz shook her head, settling her feathers back into place.

"But I—"

"MYSTICON KNIGHT!" The voice seemed even closer now.

"AAAAH!" Em shouted. She glared at Topaz. "I know you heard *that*."

Topaz twitched her shoulders in what Em could have sworn was a shrug.

"MYSTICON KNIGHT!" shouted the voice, seeming to pierce directly into Em's brain. *"HALT AND ATTEND TO ME! I AM IN NEED OF YOUR AID!"*

"Gaaaaah!" Em covered her ears with her hands. "I'm attending, I'm attending! Do you have to need my aid so loudly?" She pulled on Topaz's reins, and the confused griffin reluctantly slowed and hovered in place.

"My apologies, Knight," the voice said in a much more conversational tone, making Em sigh with relief. *"It has been centuries since anyone was able to hear me, and since I spoke to anyone save myself."*

"Oh, that's sad, I'm sorry, you must—wait, centuries?" asked Em. "You sound like a girl. How old are you? And who are you? And *where* are you? Are you invisible? And why can't my griffin hear you?" She glanced up and around, wincing. "That's a lot of questions, sorry. I don't mean to be rude. We don't get a lot of shouty disembodied voices around here."

"*Your curiosity is understandable, Knight. It is unsurprising that you do not know of me. That unfamiliarity is part of my sad tale. I will answer your questions in reverse order.*"

"Reverse order?" Em said, impressed. "Huh, I don't even remember the last question I asked."

"*Ahem. Your griffin cannot hear me for a simple reason: Your griffin is not a Mysticon. Also, I am not invisible. I am projecting my voice to you from worlds away, from my prison in the stars. A thousand years ago, a wicked curse befell the Mysticons. One of their own was taken from them, and all memory of her was magically erased. You asked who I am. I am that Mysticon, the one who was taken. I am the fifth Mysticon.*"

Em gasped. "What?!? The fifth? That's . . . that's a thing? How is that a thing?"

"*I realize this must be a shock to you. But I can prove what I say. Imani Firewing, the Mysticon Dragon Mage, is a very brave warrior.*" The voice halted, then resumed more softly. "*Was. She . . . was . . . very brave. I am sorry. I forget sometimes that a thousand years have passed, and all I knew is gone."* She continued, more briskly. *"Regardless. Imani had a secret. She was deathly afraid . . . of foz."*

Em had not been expecting that. "F-foz? The original Dragon Mage, leader of the Mysticons and wielder of the Star Dragon, had foz fear?"

"Yes. She was deeply ashamed, and revealed her phobia only to her fellow Mysticons. We guarded this secret closely, as our enemies could easily have used it against us. The sole record of it is in the Codex. And even there it is disguised, saying that Imani prefers quiet, solitary contemplation during foz season. When you leave here, check the Codex, and you will see that what I say is true."

"Hey, I actually read that! I remember because it seemed so unlike her. So *that's* why she didn't like to go out during foz season! Huh!" Em took a deep breath as the implications hit her. "Oh my goblin. There are five Mysticons? There are *five Mysticons*! But that means . . . I don't even know what that means! It means something for sure, though! Arkayna and Malvaron will know. We've gotta—" Then she caught herself, realizing something

THE SECRET OF THE FIFTH MYSTICON

else. "You've been trapped for . . . so, so long. That's awful. Why didn't you call to us before? We could have helped you!"

"My prison is held shut with a series of arcane puzzle-locks. No one in the realm is more expert with locks than I, and yet in a thousand years I was able to open only one. That loosened my bonds enough that I was able to call out to you tonight. My long study of the other locks leads me to believe that they can be opened by only the other four Mysticons working together. And you must hurry."

"Of course, we'll free you as soon as we can! But . . . why are you so worried about time?" asked Em. "It's already been a thousand years, like you said."

"And now we come to your very first question: How old am I? When I was imprisoned here, I was not much older than you are now, Knight. The prison separated my spirit from my body at that point. And while my spirit has endured, my body has long since faded. After so long, I can feel the rest of me beginning to fade as well. I would not end my time as a helpless prisoner, Mysticon Knight. I beg you, release me so that I may rest in peace, a free soul at last."

"Oh no," Em murmured. "That's so sad. . . ."

"It will be a relief," the voice said reassuringly. *"And there is a boon in it for you as well. When I am released and pass on, the Mysticon magic bound to me will also be released. A new fifth Mysticon will be called to join you and your companions. Perhaps you already know the person who will be called."*

"What? What do you mean?"

"Do you know anyone who operates quietly, from the shadows?" The voice grew more proud, remembering her past accomplishments. *"Someone who scouts ahead, so that you and the rest of your team always know exactly where to go? Who—"*

Em clapped her hands together, cutting the voice off. "Yes! *DOUG!* Doug is always helping us in the background, which is . . . shadowlike, right?"

"Well . . ." replied the voice skeptically.

Em charged over the voice's hesitation. "And he never expects anything in return, which you could definitely say is quiet. He's a quiet operator, for sure."

The voice *hmm*ed doubtfully.

But Em was on a roll. "Oh, and he told us all about Mare-Con, so we knew what to expect, just like a scout!" She put her hand to her brow as the revelation sunk in. "This is perfect. *Doug* could be the fifth Mysticon!"

In Which Much (but Not All) Is Found,
and Most (but Not All) Are Convinced

3

EM BURST INTO THE STRONGHOLD TO FIND ARKAYNA, ZARYA, Piper, Malvaron, Doug, and Choko waiting for her in front of the monitor. "Good," she panted, "you're here."

"Of *course* we're here!" said Piper, looking up from where she and Choko were playing with some toys on the floor. "You used your *most-extra-serious voice* when you called."

Em looked down at her. "Piper, why are Doug's Gnomez 2 Men collectible action figures riding on Glimmer Gust's back?"

"They're . . . going on an adventure together?" Piper swept the Twinkly Mare behind her with a guilty look. Taking the cue, Choko flopped down in front of the Gnomez 2 Men toys and spread his ears wide to hide them, blinking in fake innocence.

"I said she could, Em," Doug spoke up. "It's cool."

Em sighed. "Doug, that was *your* pres—never mind. Never mind! There's so much going on! A voice came from the sky, and she's the spirit of the fifth Mysticon, and she knows stuff that only the original Mysticons would know, and a curse trapped her in the stars and made everyone forget about her, and we have to free her fast by opening a bunch of puzzle-locks, all the Mysticons together! And at the end"—Em paused, a little out of breath—"she told me we need to search the Codex for a spell to take us to someplace called 'the Chillwaste.' That's where the locks are. So! Uh . . ."—she looked at her friends, who sat frozen, staring back at her with expressions that ranged from shock to incredulity—"what . . . do you think?"

Zarya was the first to speak. "The Chillwaste, huh?"

Choko squeaked dubiously, miming a shiver.

"It's an ice dimension," said Em. "That's all I know about it so far."

"It's an ice dimension with *puzzles*!" Piper said. "I'm in!"

"Hold on," said Arkayna. "'In'? No one is 'in' anything yet. I have a *lot* of questions."

"So do I," agreed Malvaron.

"Okay," Em said, "we can ask her when we get there! Let's find that spell!"

"I think I'd rather ask her first," Arkayna said. "Where were you when you heard the voice?"

"Flying over Magi Mall, but—"

"Arkayna's right," Malvaron said. "We need to know more before we go jumping around to ice dimensions."

"Well, uh, you won't be able to hear the voice anyway," Em explained. "Only Mysticons can hear her. Sorry."

"All right, then," Arkayna said. "Malvaron, you stay here with Doug and search the Codex. We'll go talk to this 'fifth Mysticon.'" She stood up and motioned to Zarya and Piper. "Girls? It's magic hour!"

A little while later, all four of the Mysticons were suited up and flying back and forth over Magi Mall on their griffins, and things were feeling decidedly unmagical.

"Hello?" Em called, over and over again. "Hello, are you there?" But no one answered.

"What, did she get shy or something?" Zarya asked impatiently. "Where is this girl?"

"I don't know," admitted Em.

Forming her hands into a cone around her mouth, Piper hooted at the sky. *"Helloooooooo! Old cursed Mysticon-girl-spirit-thingy! Where aaaaaaare yoooooooou?"*

Em looked pained. "Piper, don't be rude!"

Piper dropped her hands. "Sorry. But what am I supposed to call her?"

"Call her . . . oh my goblin. I forgot to ask her name! Oh, I'm so embarrassed. No wonder she's not answering!"

Arkayna scanned the sky, looking for anything out of the ordinary. "Em, I'm sure she doesn't think you're rude."

"I dunno," muttered Em. "She was a little touchy." She raised her voice. "I'm super-sorry we didn't introduce

ourselves properly, but we're all here to meet you now! . . .
Hello?"

Nothing.

"She's gone for now, at least," Arkayna decided. "Let's
head back and see what the Codex has to say."

Back at the Stronghold, while Choko dozed in the pile of
Gnomez 2 Men toys, the four Mysticons crowded around
the Codex, reading the spell that Malvaron and Doug had
found.

"This looks pretty straightforward, at least," said
Arkayna. "Just a simple portal spell with a few extra flour-
ishes thrown in to get us to the right dimension."

"And it says right here," Em said, pointing excitedly to
the page, "that the Chillwaste is an icy prison that can
be found only using this spell. See? She knew what she
was talking about, which means she was real, which
means I didn't imagine it!"

"Who said you imagined it?" asked Zarya, raising her
eyebrows.

"Uh . . . no one," said Em, blushing. "But I'm very, very relieved anyway. Whoo! Let's go!"

"Just a minute," Arkayna said, holding up a hand. "This doesn't make sense. Why would a Mysticon be imprisoned using a spell in the Codex, which is a book only Mysticons have access to?"

"Well, she did say it was a curse," Em replied thoughtfully. "So maybe there was trickery involved. I bet the curse turned the original Mysticons' magic back on them!"

"Ooooh, that's so *sneaky*!" said Piper. "I can't wait to find out who cursed her so we can *get* 'em! Quick, let's get her out so we can ask her!"

"The person who cursed her is probably long gone by now, Piper," Malvaron pointed out. "This would have happened centuries ago."

Zarya leaned forward, eyes widening in excitement. "If it even *was* a person. It could have been an immortal monster. Or an undead skeleton, like Dreadbane! Or—"

"Oooooooh!" squealed Piper. "I gotta know!"

"Slow down, girls," said Arkayna. "I'm looking at the

spell right here, and it doesn't say anything about a curse or a memory wipe. It's just a portal, that's all."

Malvaron nodded. "And we still haven't decided—"

"Arkayna," Zarya cut in. "This girl is a Mysticon, and she needs our help. Are we really gonna leave her to fade away to nothing in a place called 'the Chillwaste'?"

"And *you said* the book wasn't telling you anything, right?" Piper asked. "So the only way to know is to go ask her. Riiiight?"

"She did say there were a *bunch* of locks," said Em. "So there'll be time to talk about all kinds of things while we're trying to free her. And, hey, if we get there and don't like what we see, we just jump back here, right?"

Arkayna looked at Malvaron.

Malvaron smiled. "I gotta say, they're making some good points. And I *am* curious."

Arkayna sighed. "All right."

"Yesssss," said Em.

"Awesome," said Zarya, nodding.

Piper cartwheeled across the floor. "Woo-hooooooo! Let's do it!"

Arkayna picked up the Codex and walked to a clear

patch of floor. With her staff, she drew the first glyph of the portal spell. The glyph hung in the air, glowing green, as Arkayna began to recite, *"Attend to my summons, attend to—"*

"STOP!" shouted Em.

Arkayna jumped and whirled around, causing the glyph to spark and then fade. "What? Why?"

"Yeah, Em," said Zarya, "you looked like you were all ready to go. Did you remember something else that you just *have* to take to an icy prison dimension?"

"Not something. Some*one.*" Em turned to Doug. The cyclops was watching quietly from one side of the room, sipping on his tea. "You have to come with us," Em told him.

The *crash* of the teacup hitting the floor was almost drowned out by Malvaron, Arkayna, Piper, and Zarya exclaiming in unison, *"What?"*

In Which Eyes, Minds,

and a Portal Are Opened, in That Order

"... AND YOU TOLD US ALL ABOUT MARE-CON, JUST LIKE A scout, which is just what the fifth Mysticon would do! See? It all fits!" Em finished her case for the parallels between Doug and the spirit's description of the fifth Mysticon.

Doug stood slack-jawed. For a moment, the only sound was Choko lapping up the spreading puddle of tea at the cyclops's feet.

Em walked over to him. "Doug, you have to be there when we free the fifth Mysticon's spirit. The magic will be able to call someone new, to choose a *new* Mysticon, and I think it'll choose you!"

Doug shook his head. "Em, that's so nice of you. I don't even know what to say. But I don't feel like a Mysticon. At all."

Em chuckled. "You think *I* did? Hex no!" She turned to Arkayna. "Did you feel like you could be a Mysticon before the Dragon Disk called you?"

"Not at all," Arkayna admitted. "All I wanted was to be more normal."

"What about you, Zarya?" asked Em.

"I mean"—Zarya smirked—"I knew I was awesome. But I didn't know I was *this* awesome."

"Piper?"

Piper burst out laughing wildly.

"I'll take that as a no." Em turned back to Doug. "See?"

Doug looked around at them, eye wide. "Well, if you really think I should come . . ."

Arkayna opened her mouth to speak, but Em cut her off with an emphatic: "We do!"

"Oh man, oh man." Doug glanced down at himself. "I

guess I better go pack! Don't worry. I'll be quick!" He ran off to his room.

As soon as he was out of earshot, the other Mysticons and Malvaron all turned to Em.

"Why would you—?" started Arkayna.

"Are you sure—?" asked Malvaron.

"This is weird . . ." muttered Zarya.

"This is great!" hooted Piper.

"Listen," hissed Em, silencing them with a gesture. "Who, besides us, knows more about what it takes to actually be a Mysticon than Doug? Who always has our backs? Doug. Who's always helping us train? *Doug.* Who is just as dedicated as we are? *Doug!* Right?"

The other four nodded, none more enthusiastically than Piper.

"So if someone else is going to join the team," Em said, "who else would you want it to be? Who else *could* it be?"

"Huh," said Zarya. "I didn't think about it like that."

"Me neither," chirped Piper. "This is even greater than I thought!"

"All right," Arkayna said reluctantly. "I mean, it sounds like the Chillwaste is just ice and puzzles. Doug will be fine." She turned to Malvaron. "Right? He'll be fine?"

Malvaron thought for a moment, then said, "I actually have something to help with that. Be right back!" He jogged out of the room just as Doug staggered in with a huge pack on his back.

"I didn't know what I'd need," Doug said, "so I brought a little of everything."

Piper walked a slow circle around him, nodding. "Uh-huh. Uh-huh. That looks like everything, all right." Then she held up the Glimmer Gust doll. "Room for this?"

"Sure." Eager to please, Doug took the doll, wrapped it carefully in a bit of cloth, and tucked it away in a side pouch. Choko climbed up Doug's leg and onto the pack, tugging straps, checking buckles, and poking at bulges. When he was fully satisfied, he hopped onto Doug's head. Leaning down into the cyclops's eyeline, he gave Doug a supportive chirp and a thumbs-up.

Malvaron came hustling back to the group, a pile of leather and glass in his hands making an odd tinkling noise. "This is a special project I've been working on for myself," he told Doug, "but I think you should have it." He unfolded the bundle into a long belt with several dangling loops. Each loop held a potion bottle securely in place. "Take off your pack for a minute."

With a grunt, Doug unshouldered his pack and dropped it to the floor, then dipped his head toward the ground so Choko could hop off. Malvaron reached up and placed the belt over Doug's neck and around one of his arms, so the colorful row of potions hung within easy reach across his body.

"All right, you've got everything you might need here," Malvaron said, rubbing his hands together as he admired his handiwork. He reached out and tapped a few of the potions in turn. "Here's Titan Strength; it'll make you even more of a beast than you are now. Here's True Aim, in case you have to hit someone at a distance. Here's—"

"Whoa, whoa, whoa," Doug protested, holding out his hands. "Who am I going to be hitting?"

"You never know," said Malvaron with a shrug. He tapped at his phone a few times, and Doug's phone beeped in response. "Anyway, I just glyphed you the whole list. Everything is color-coded; it should be easy. Just remember the number one rule of potions. . . ." He trailed off, raising his eyebrows expectantly at Doug. "Come on, say it with me, man!"

Doug obediently chimed in as he and Malvaron chorused, *"Don't mix anything. Ever."*

"You're gonna do great," Malvaron said proudly. "Fist bump for luck!"

Doug grinned as he bumped fists with Malvaron. Em, looking on, beamed with joy.

"Are we ready?" asked Arkayna.

"Ready!" Em said.

"Sure," said Zarya.

"I repeat: Let's do it!" Piper said, turning another cartwheel.

The four girls and Malvaron turned to look at Doug. After a moment, Choko elbowed Doug in the ankle and cleared his throat conspicuously.

"Oh! Yeah! I'm ready!" Doug stammered, hefting his pack onto his back again.

"All right, here we go," Arkayna said as she began drawing glyphs in the air. One by one, the glyphs glowed green and shifted through the air until they formed a large oval. While she drew, Arkayna chanted,

"Attend to my summons, attend to
my knocks,
Unlock the door that will lead to
more locks,
Take us to faraway ice with all haste,
Open the way and reveal: the
Chillwaste!"

On the last word, the glyphs flared from green to white, and the center of the oval turned an opaque, sparkling gray and began to swirl. Em felt tendrils of cold air touch her forehead, her hands, her neck. She shivered.

Arkayna turned to look over her shoulder, her hair lifting in the breeze from the portal. "This is it! On three?"

Together the four girls and Doug chanted, "One . . . two . . . *THREE!*"

They jumped in and were swallowed by the swirling magic.

*In Which the Team Goes Down
and the Stakes Go Up*

5

"SO THIS IS THE CHILLWASTE," DOUG SAID, LOOKING AROUND.

"It sure is, uh . . ."

"Boring," Piper finished with an exaggerated sigh. With the swirling portal at their backs, the five of them stared across an endless plane of white. The unbroken sheet of ice ran all the way to the horizon, glowing with a soft light from within. Above them, the night sky was a deep, unbroken black.

"I was gonna say 'sleek,'" Doug said.

"The elf is correct," came a wavering voice, seemingly

from right next to the Mysticons. They all jumped and shouted in surprise.

"Could you just . . . not . . . *do* that?" Em panted, taking deep breaths to regain her calm. "But, wait. You all heard that, right?"

The others nodded. Em looked to Doug. "Even you?" Doug nodded again, eye wide. Em felt unexpected relief rush through her. "Oh, thank the stars," she breathed. It wasn't that she had doubted, she told herself, but it *was* lonely when you were the only one who had heard a spooky voice. Much better to have friends who were right there with you. Another thought struck, and she craned her neck to study the black sky. "Hey, speaking of stars! Uh, fifth Mysticon? Didn't you say you were trapped in the stars? Are we in the right place?"

"Indeed you are, Knight, as otherwise your large friend would not be able to hear me." The voice seemed to drift to a new position behind them, on the far side of the portal. *"You have not seen all there is to see."*

Em followed the voice, balancing carefully on the slippery ice as she made her way around the shimmering oval. "Oh, this is Doug! He's the one I was telling you about. He—oh." She pulled up short as she saw the view that the portal had been blocking. Almost at her feet, the ice cracked, revealing dark brown, nearly black rock beneath. The crack widened as it got farther from her, forming a deep, jagged chasm, lit by veins of shining ice running through the dark, rocky walls. In the patch of sky directly above the chasm, a group of stars glowed brightly.

"Above is my prison," whispered the voice, *"and below are the locks. Please, Mysticons . . . and Doug. Make haste. Descend and begin!"*

"Hi, wait . . . ," stammered Arkayna, tottering over to join Em and trying desperately not to fall. "Before we do anything, we have so many questions for you. Like, why—*aaaaaAAAAAAH!*" Her feet went out from under her, and she landed hard on her backside. "Ow."

"All will be revealed, Dragon Mage," replied the voice. *"There is no time now. I feel myself growing weak."*

"But can't you at least tell us—"

"Sooooo weeeeak." The voice grew fainter, and fainter still. *"Make haaaaaste."*

"Hello?" Arkayna asked. "Are you still there?" With Em's help, and using her staff to steady her, Arkayna carefully got to her feet. They listened, but there was no response. "Oh, bugbears. That was—"

"Convenient," said Zarya. She and Doug shuffled gingerly around the portal to join them. "Guess she didn't want to talk."

"But she told us where the puzzles are, right?" Piper asked as she glided around the portal, nimbly sliding her feet across the ice and pushing herself forward. Turning gracefully, she pointed her feet wide and drifted in a lazy circle around her friends. "Let's go find the puzzles!"

Em raised her eyebrows and smiled. "Piper, you're really good at that."

"What, this?" Piper looked down at her feet skimming across the ice. "I just picked it up somewhere, I guess. Wanna learn? After puzzles?"

Em chuckled. "Sure. After puzzles."

"Deal!" Piper grinned.

The five of them traveled to where the crack in the ice began. Here, the ground was dark stone. Arkayna breathed a sigh of relief as she stepped onto it. Em caught her eye, and they shared a quick smile. With Arkayna in the lead, the five of them descended into the narrow ravine created by the crack. The path dropped steeply, and soon the rock-and-ice walls towered above them. The slice of sky they could see grew thinner and thinner, until it almost touched the small patch of stars on either side.

Then, abruptly, the walls opened out to either side of them. They found themselves in a canyon in the shape of a huge triangle. They had emerged from the middle of one side, and opposite them the canyon's walls came together to form a point. Gigantic, triangular, horizontally striped pillars rose out of the ground, randomly spread across the space. Sections of the pillars were made of brown rock, other stripes were glowing white ice, and others were . . .

"Is that gold?" asked Doug.

"Looks like it," Em replied.

Zarya laughed. "What kind of chasm has . . . bling?"

"This has to be the first puzzle," Arkayna said. She moved to the nearest pillar, making a gesture with her staff so that the green orb at its top glowed brightly. She held the light toward the striped column and inspected its surface. The ice making up the bottom stripe reached to just above her head and seemed featureless. Above the ice, on the second stripe, the dark rock looked similarly blank. "Everyone look around. Maybe there's writing on one of these, or some other kind of marking. And be careful; we don't know what's safe to touch."

Doug obediently stuffed his hands in his pockets. "No touching. Gotcha. I'll look over he—"

"Ooh, the ice is cold!" yelped Piper, her hands flat against the white bottom section of another pillar. "I wonder if the gold is warm!" She ran off to a third pillar where the bottom stripe shone a buttery yellow.

"Piper," called Em, "that seems like maybe not a great idea?"

But it was too late. "This game is gonna be fab-*tacular*, I can tell!" Piper shouted. She skidded to a halt and held her hands out to the gold.

As soon as Piper's gloves made contact, the gold sections on all the monoliths lit up. A low, grating sound echoed through the cavern as the columns ground into movement. The sound resolved into a resonant hum as the columns began to rotate in place.

Piper clapped delightedly. "I did it!" Then she tipped her head to the side and pondered the spinning pillars. "What'd I do?"

A deeper *boom* came from one side of the triangular chasm, and all five of them spun to face it. As they watched, the wall on that side of the valley moved! It pivoted from the closed point opposite the entrance and, with a loud scraping noise, moved a few feet toward them before grinding to a halt. Now the area they stood in was a slightly asymmetrical smaller triangle.

Zarya walked over to sling an arm around Piper's shoulders. "I've got good news and bad news. The good news is, I just figured out part of this puzzle. Specifically, I figured out what happens if we fail."

Em stared up at the wall. Stray pebbles and a shower of pulverized ice pattered down from the faraway top. "What?"

"That's the bad news," Zarya said. "We get smooshed."

In Which Everything Is Loud

6

"OKAY!" ARKAYNA SHOUTED, SPREADING HER ARMS WIDE in warning. "No more touching things! For real this time!"

Em nodded vigorously, still staring up at the wall that was now just a bit closer to her. Then she noticed Zarya and Piper pointing at some of the columns and whispering to each other. "Hey, uh, Zarya? Piper? Did you hear what Arkayna said?"

"Yeah, it was hard to miss," Zarya replied. "But c'mere and look at this."

Em, Arkayna, and Doug went to stand by Zarya and Piper.

"See how the gold parts of some of these line up?" Zarya gestured at two nearby pillars, then a third, then a fourth. "I know you're not gonna like this, Arkayna, but I think we gotta move these around."

"Yeah, they're gonna make a picture!" agreed Piper. "It's gonna be sweeeeeet!"

Arkayna squinted. "That makes sense, actually." Then she looked dubiously at the base of the nearest pillar. "But how are we going to move them? They're huge, and now they're spinning."

"Well," said Zarya with a shrug, "we could try just pushing them." Seeing Arkayna's concerned look, she added, "We have to try *something*."

Em nodded. "Zarya's right, Arkayna. Let's try *carefully* pushing just one and see what happens."

"All right," Arkayna agreed. She moved closer to the pillar Piper had touched, holding out her staff again. Leaning forward, she furrowed her brow as she peered at the smooth yellow surface of its bottom stripe. "I just wish we could find some kind of hints about—"

"Whoa, look out!" called Doug. He pulled Arkayna backward as one of the edges of the triangular pillars spun into the space where she had just been. Arkayna's arm flew out as she fell back, and the top of her staff glanced off the pillar's surface.

WHAAAAAAAANG! The orb of Arkayna's staff flashed green as it impacted the gold, and the noise of the collision seemed to be amplified many times over. With a rumble, the pillar began to move away from Arkayna! It trundled across the open space, the ground seeming to part before it and then re-form in its wake, until it collided with another column.

"Way to go!" Piper grinned. "I bet—"

BOOM. Scraaaaaaaape. The wall moved again on its pivot, grinding a few feet closer.

"Oh," Em realized. "It closes in every time we do *any-thing*?" She did some quick calculations, looking back and forth between the walls. "We need a plan here. We've got maybe a few dozen moves to play with, and there are a dozen of these things to line up."

"Let's spread out," decided Arkayna. "We'll look at this from all angles and see what kind of picture the gold sections will make. Then we'll figure out where to start."

The five of them took up positions all around the chasm, trying to figure out how to align the gold pieces. After a minute, another *BOOM* sounded, and the wall moved in on them again.

Zarya shook her head. "You were half right, Em. The wall closes in when we do anything, *and* when we do nothing. I can't make any kind of real picture, but I think we should just try to make all the gold parts of each pillar touch and see what happens."

Piper nodded. "I can kinda see it making a sort of blobby, curvy, spiky . . . thing? I'm sure it'll get clearer as we go. Let's start with this one!" She pointed at a pillar near the entrance.

"Hey, I don't know if this is right, but . . ." Doug trailed off.

"No, Doug, what is it?" said Em.

"Shouldn't we move all the pillars away from the wall that's moving? That'll give us the most time to—"

"He's right!" exclaimed Piper. "Arkayna, bring your shoving stick over here!"

As Arkayna hurried across to Piper's column, Em frowned. "It doesn't make sense that Arkayna has to move all of them herself," she muttered. "What if . . ." She gave the pillar next to her an experimental shove as a corner of it rotated by her. Nothing happened. "Hmmmmmm . . . The staff flared up when it hit the pillar. I don't have a staff, but maybe if I use *my* magic . . ." She held up a hand and summoned her pink shield. As the next corner of the pillar went by, Em gave it a hard *whap* with the shield.

WHAAAAAAAANG! The pillar sailed across the valley, stopping between two other columns.

BOOM. Scraaaaaaaaaape. The wall shifted closer. Now it was within five feet of the pillar Arkayna and Piper stood by.

Piper looked back at the wall and then over at Em. "I wanna try!" she decided. She jumped in front of Arkayna, who had already started to raise her staff. "C'mon, Hoopy, don't let me down!" Piper shouted, summoning one of her golden Mysticon Energy Hoops. She tossed the ring at the huge column.

WHAAAAAAAANG! As the column started to move away from her, Piper did a little dance in celebration. "Go, Hoopy!" she chanted. "Go, Hoopy! Go—oop!"

A *BOOM* cut her off. Piper skipped away, Arkayna on her heels, as the wall ground even closer.

"All right, let's do this!" Zarya summoned her Mysticon bow and nocked a magic blue arrow, aiming at the next pillar.

Doug looked anxiously around as the *WHAAAAANG* of Zarya's arrow hitting the pillar echoed all around them. "I feel like a fifth leg on a griffin," he said. "I wish I could help somehow."

Em hurried to reassure him. "Maybe you can! The pillars are responding to Mysticon magic, sure, but maybe they would move for any helpful magic. Why not try a potion?"

Doug pulled an orange, glowing vial off of the belt Malvaron gave him. "This one *is* for Titan Strength," he mused.

Em nodded. "Perfect!" She smiled encouragingly and gave him a big thumbs-up.

In one gulp, Doug downed the contents of the vial. A second later, a ripple of orange energy seemed to flow over him. "Whoa," he said, "I feel . . . helpful!" He grinned. "Titanically helpful!" He took a deep breath and gave a nearby pillar a huge shove. To his and Em's delight, it moved a few feet . . . but then it stopped again.

"Okay, so not *as* good as Mysticon magic," Doug said.

"But plenty good enough!" Em said. "Let's get this puzzle solved!"

Together, and—between the magical impacts and the grinding pillars and the booming, scraping wall and the group's shouted instructions to one another—with a *lot* of noise, the team assembled the pillars into a line against the non-moving side of the chasm. As Zarya's arrow careened off the last pillar and shifted it into place, the five of them let out a cheer. The gold sections were all lined up and touching!

Em squinted up at the resulting shape. It was, she thought, just like Piper had described: a blobby, curvy, spiky . . . thing. Not what she would have chosen for a puzzle solution, but then again—

Another *BOOM* echoed through the cavern. They turned to watch as the far wall pivoted and scraped closer again . . . and completely covered the way they had come in.

The puzzle was still unsolved, Em realized. And now they were trapped.

In Which Perspective Shifts and Stars Align

7

"OHHHHHH MY GOBLIN," SAID EM. "THIS IS BAD."

"Look on the bright side," Piper chirped. "The way out was in the very middle of the wall, and it just got covered up now. That means we've still got half our moves left!"

"Huh," Doug said. "So we're only halfway to being doomed?"

"Don't get too bright-eyed," Zarya put in. "Everything is still very, *very* not cool."

"Wait." Arkayna held out a hand to quiet them, staring

up at the pillars. "'Don't get too bright-eyed,' you said. I think you're onto something!"

"Oh . . . kay?" Zarya arched a skeptical eyebrow.

"No, really!" Arkayna said. "What if the gold isn't what we should be paying attention to? The gold and the ice are both glowing; what if the trick is to *ignore* them?"

"Ohhh," breathed Em, picking up on the idea. "We look at the gold and white together as the background color, and we try to make a picture with the brown rock!"

They all stared up at the pillars again, this time paying close attention to the rocky sections. Doug *hmm*ed thoughtfully, using his finger to trace a shape in the air. "Does it have to be a picture? What if it's a letter?"

"Huh?" asked Piper. She ran over to Doug and tried to find a place to look where she could line up his moving finger with the pillars. "You're too tall!" she cried, hopping up and down. "Come down here and do that!"

Doug ducked down and traced the shape again, reaching out in front of Piper so she could see.

"He's right!" she said. "It's an *M*!"

Em gasped. Now she could see it, too—they were only

a handful of moves away from the rock forming the curves and slash of the Gemina letter *M*. "That has to be it! *M* for *Mysticons*!"

With Doug calling out instructions, the girls bashed and whapped and twanged their Mysticon weapons against the pillars again. The booming, moving wall got closer and closer, but soon Piper whipped her hoop at one last column, which ground into place with a satisfying *THUD*. At that moment, the pillars quickly rotated one last time and, with a series of *chunk*ing sounds, locked into place with their flat sides aligned, forming a solid wall of gold, ice, and rock. The shining gold and the glowing white ice flared even more brightly, outlining the brown *M* in stark contrast. Then the wall of columns began to slowly sink into the earth.

"This is so *cool*!" giggled Piper.

"This is good," Em agreed. Then, more hesitantly: "This is good, right?"

"It must be," sighed Arkayna.

"I'm not relaxing until we know what happens next," muttered Zarya.

"Uh, well, good news!" Doug spoke up. "You can relax!" Then he pointed a finger upward regretfully. "But, bad news? The walls are closing in again."

The girls looked up in alarm to where the stars glittered between the walls of the now very skinny triangular chasm. Sure enough, while the one side had stopped moving toward them, the tops of both walls were now beginning to change and shift. While they watched, the rock and ice seemed to reach toward the stars from both directions.

Then, as they watched, fingers of ice grew outward from the canyon walls. But instead of obscuring the stars as they formed, the icy protrusions . . . moved the stars! The ice grew, and the stars obediently shifted out of the way, clustering closer together in their shrinking patch of sky.

"Whaaaaaaat the hex?" whispered Zarya. Em had no answer for her.

Its job seemingly done, the ice withdrew into the sides of the chasm. And then, to everyone's relief, the moving wall began to recede, pivoting back the way it had come. The path they had traveled came back into view. With one final grinding noise, the wall shifted out of the way even farther, and another path appeared in the point opposite the entrance.

The Mysticons and Doug stared up at the sky in wonder. The cluster of lights above them was definitely a different shape. They had actually moved the stars! Finally Piper broke the silence.

"That . . . was . . . *amazing*!" she cried. "Quick, let's go find the next puzzle!" She ran off toward the new path, shouting back over her shoulder, "Best ice dimension *ever*!"

Em smiled. She had to agree.

In Which Our Heroes Break the Oldest Rule

8

AT FIRST, THE NEW PATH LOOKED MUCH LIKE THE OLD ONE. Glowing ice veins traveled with them along a narrow, rocky ravine that twisted and curved back on itself. Then the Mysticons and Doug turned one particularly sharp corner, and the scenery changed.

The path ended in a small, rough circle. In the center of the open space was a statue of the original Mysticons, just like the one they had all seen in the palace treasury . . . but this version was made entirely of shining ice.

Past the statue, passages forked off to the left and

right. And between those two passages, the normally uneven rock wall was smooth and velvety. The veins of ice, instead of shooting randomly through the rock, converged here and formed a large rectangular frame. Shifting colors, the ice then spidered inward to create a picture inside the frame.

"Heyyyyy," said Zarya as she looked at the image appreciatively, "looks like the original Mysticons liked to smash orcs, too. I gotta try that net-arrow thing!"

Indeed, the picture showed the original Mysticons beating back an entire horde of orcs. At the far left, the tall human form of the first Mysticon Ranger stood alert on a rocky spire, his eyes locked on the arrow he had just fired. The arrow trailed a spidery, glowing energy web behind it. The web was about to drop on a whole cluster of orcs, who looked up in dismay. Above him, the elven Mysticon Striker somersaulted through the air. She was tossing her golden hoops at a few orcs attempting to claw their way up the spire toward the Ranger.

"Awwwww, look at the old me, looking out for the old you," Piper said to Zarya, pointing in excitement. "Striker and Ranger, buds forever!" Piper and Zarya grinned and high-fived.

Below and to the right of the Ranger, the original Mysticon Dragon Mage fired her dragon bracer at the horde, her mouth open in a triumphant shout. The blue Dragon avatar streaked out of the bracer and across the battlefield, orcs fleeing from it in terror.

"She looks so commanding," said Arkayna.

Em caught the hint of wistfulness in her friend's voice and hurried to reassure her. "You look like that all the time!"

Arkayna smiled at Em. "Thanks." Then she pointed to the center of the frame, where the first Mysticon Knight swung his glowing two-handed sword in a wide arc, colliding directly with the breastplate of the largest orc. "Original you is kicking some serious butt. But I bet you could take that orc, too. Easy."

Em looked more closely at the broadsword. "Interesting technique," she decided, "but I'll stick with my shield."

"Hey, I have a question," Doug said, peering at the right side of the image. "This . . . doesn't look like an orc."

The Mysticons hurried to join Doug, and Em gasped. "You're right! That must be her!"

Descending on the back line of orcs was a fifth figure, a nimble dwarf wearing a gold headpiece and a lithe black outfit with gold trim. In each hand, she held a flaming dagger, ready to attack the unsuspecting orcs from behind.

The girls studied the dwarven figure for a moment. Then Arkayna turned to look Doug appraisingly up and down, and the cyclops sucked in air between his teeth. "Oooh," he muttered, "I think I'm too tall for that suit."

"Gotta say," said Zarya, "I never thought of you as a dagger guy."

"Oh," Doug said. "You might be right."

"Well, but!" said Em. "The original Knight used a broadsword, and I don't. You don't *have* to use daggers."

Doug brightened up a bit. "Okay. That's good. Maybe I'm more of a slingshot guy. Or a 'stern talking-to' guy, even?"

"Look at all the shiny on her head!" Piper put in. "That thing looks *serious*!"

"But it's not a tiara, like the Dragon Mage headpiece," Arkayna said, tapping the crown on her own head. "It's more for her face. Look how it comes down to frame her eyes."

"Ooh, maybe it's another weapon!" said Em. "Like, maybe she can shoot eyeblasts with it. Doug, that would be perfect for you!"

"Darn rootin' tootin'!" agreed Piper. "Your eyeblast would be like *booooosh!*" She mimed being caught in an energy wave from Doug's direction, stumbling backward until she hit the back of the ice sculpture. Dramatically, she plastered herself against the outcropping between the Ranger and the Dragon Mage, as if she were being smashed flat. "And the bad guys would be all *aaaaaaack!*" She stuck her tongue out and slid down the statue, rolling her eyes back in her head.

"The real question," Zarya said, "is why is she *here*"—she pointed to the sneaky dwarf's image on the wall—"and not *there.*" She pointed at the sculpture.

"She's not on the original statue eith—" Em started.

"Right," Zarya said, "but I'm saying why remake that statue here, as part of her prison? What's the point of showing the fifth Mysticon in one place but not the other?"

"Maybe the person who built this place is taunting her," said Em sadly. "Reminding her that even though she fought with the team, she didn't get included in their history."

"Owwww . . ." Piper complained, getting up and rubbing her lower back. "This thing is *pointy*." She leaned forward to inspect the outcropping more closely. "Hey, c'mere, check this out!"

The rest of them hurried over to Piper, who began climbing on and around the jutting ice, shifting her feet around to different poses. "Piper," said Arkayna, "what the dragon patties are you *doing*?"

"Look!" Piper replied, lifting up one foot to show them. "There are some super-rough patches on this part! And I thought, hey, if I were a fifth Mysticon and I was gonna be on this statue, where would I be? And there *is* this big empty space right in the middle by these stairs, and"— Piper stabbed a thumb back toward the image on the wall—"she looks kinda crouchy and bendy, and I was wondering, if I put my feet and hands where the rough parts are . . ." She struck another pose, up on her toes at the tip of the spire, one hand splayed on the ice in front of her for balance. "Maybe something like this?"

Em's eyes went wide. "You're saying she used to be on the statue and got taken off?"

Piper shrugged. "Maybe!"

"If the curse was designed to erase *all* record of her," Arkayna mused, "maybe it altered the statue magically? But why would the magic leave a trace like . . . Wait. She's here. Like, actually here! Why aren't we asking her?" She tipped her head back toward the stars. "Hello?" she called. Then louder: "Hel-*lo*?"

"Oh no," Em said. "She must still be too weak to answer. We have to hurry!" She turned from side to side, looking down each of the new paths in turn. "Which way?"

After a few dozen feet, the trail to the left suddenly disappeared in a thick mist. Down to the right, they could make out colossal figures of some kind looming over the path, before the ravine took a sharp turn out of sight.

"That mist looks spooooooooky," said Piper.

"Not a fan, huh?" replied Zarya.

"I mean," Piper said, a hint of defensiveness in her voice, "it's fine. What's bad about mist? It's just water, and air, and . . . and mist! Let's go! Let's go right now!" She started off to the left.

"Aw, come on, Piper," said Zarya, following her. "I didn't mean it like that."

Meanwhile, Arkayna was peering at the figures down the right-hand path. "Is that one on the left . . . a unicorn? Kind of charging out of the wall?"

"I think so. And I think the one facing us is a wolf, maybe with something in its mouth? I can't quite make it out. It's . . . shiny?" Em said. The two of them drifted down the path, squinting.

Doug was left behind by the statue. "Uh, hey, I feel like splitting up is a bad idea," he called.

"It's okay, Doug," Arkayna said over her shoulder. "I just want to see . . ." Her voice trailed off as she went back to concentrating on the huge carvings.

"But it's the oldest rule of adventuring!" Doug said. He turned toward Zarya. "You know this, from *Remembered Realms*!"

"He's right," Zarya said, running forward a couple of

steps to catch up with Piper. Zarya reached out for the little elf, continuing, "Never split the par—"

She was cut off as the mist seemed to reach out. Swiftly, silently, it closed around Zarya and Piper and swallowed them both.

Doug gasped in shock. "Zarya? . . . Piper?" There was no answer. "They disappeared!" he yelled to Em and Arkayna.

But it was too late. Em and Arkayna had wandered too far down the path. As they turned to look at Doug, the unicorn statue's horn glowed a deep red. *Fwoom!* A thin beam of energy streaked from it right toward them!

In Which There Is a Blast, and Also the Past

9

"HORNBEAM!" DOUG SHOUTED, POINTING.

Em whipped her head around and saw the danger. In an eyeblink, she grabbed Arkayna close and raised her arm, summoning her shield. With a loud *crackle* and *sizzle*, the beam hit the shield. As energy continued to pour out of the unicorn's horn, Em grunted from the effort of holding the beam back, but she kept her shield up, deflecting the laser into the nearby wall and shearing a smoking line into the cliff.

"Get out of there!" called Doug, running toward them.

"Good thought!" Em yelled back over the crackling beam. "Arkayna, stay behind me!"

"I can shoot the horn from here," said Arkayna, charging up her staff. "I bet that would—"

"No, it has to be everyone together, remember?" Doug reminded her, pulling on her arm. "We can't do this puzzle without Piper and Zarya!"

Arkayna nodded, and the three of them fell back, using the shield as cover. When they had gone a dozen steps, the laser faltered and died, and the unicorn's horn dimmed until it was indistinguishable from the other dark rock.

Doug put one of his big hands on each of their shoulders and bowed his head, breathing deeply. "That was close," he said, relieved. "Sorry I yelled something weird at you; I just opened my mouth and that's what came out."

"What, 'hornbeam'?" Em said, chuckling. "I knew exactly what you meant. It was perfect."

"Yeah," agreed Arkayna, "weird, maybe, a little. But perfect. And thanks for keeping us from going too far in the first place. I'm glad you have our backs."

Doug's face reddened as he broke into a pleased smile.

Em's heart skipped a beat as it hit her: Doug had supported them from the background, just like the fifth Mysticon said! She took a breath to point this out, but then she hesitated, worried about spoiling the moment. She settled for grinning and patting Doug's hand on her shoulder.

The three of them turned to the misty path. "Zarya?" shouted Arkayna. *"PIPER?"* There was no answer.

"The mist just sort of . . . ate them," Doug said with a shudder. "Piper was right. It was spooky."

"We have to get them out of there!" Arkayna paced back and forth at the mouth of the path, twisting the handle of her staff. "But how do we fight mist?"

"Oh, rust," Em sighed. "I have a thought, but even I don't like the thought I'm having. Um. The mist. Did it . . ." Em swallowed, then continued. "Did it look like it hurt them?"

"No, actually," said Doug. "They just looked surprised. Not like 'Aah, a monster!' surprised. More like 'What am I looking at?' surprised, you know? And then they were gone."

"What is it, Em?" asked Arkayna.

Wincing, Em looked up at her. "I think we have to go in after them."

Arkayna stopped dead in her tracks. "What? We let the mist eat us, *too*? Don't we fail the puzzle, then?"

"I don't think the puzzle is defeating the mist," Em said. "I think the puzzle is *in* the mist."

Arkayna stared at the soupy whiteness. It swirled and eddied, offering no clues. "What if you're wrong?"

"I mean, I could be," Em said softly. "I just . . ."

Doug nodded. "I think you're right, though. And besides, we're still split up right now. If we go in, at least we'll all be in the same place. But if we're gonna jump in there, could we . . ." He trailed off, then looked down at them sheepishly. "Could we hold hands?"

"Uh, yeah we could!" said Em. "Are you kidding? I was going to ask the same thing!" She held her hands out to either side of her. Arkayna took one, Doug the other, and together the three of them marched down the narrow path. As they neared the mist, Em asked, "Ready?"

"Ready," said Arkayna.

"Oh, man," murmured Doug, but then he set his shoulders and said firmly, "Ready."

They plunged straight into the haze, which seemed to close over them eagerly. For a moment, all Em could see was white. She was glad to feel Arkayna's and Doug's hands in hers, and squeezed them in what she hoped was reassurance. Before they could squeeze back, the whiteness started to lift. Outlines became visible as her vision cleared further, and it was obvious that they were no longer in the ravine.

Under their feet was a polished, expertly crafted, dark marble floor. Directly in front of them, a round, two-tiered fountain trickled softly. Short stairways flanked the fountain, meeting in a wide landing behind it, then arcing off to hallways in either direction. The wall on the far side of the landing was dominated by the curves of a gigantic, arching stained-glass window, a window that looked strangely—

"By the Hammer of Harmon!" Em gasped. "This is the Stronghold!"

"I knew this fountain looked familiar," mused Doug. "I broke it. With my butt."

Arkayna spun around. Behind them were the floor-to-ceiling bookshelves they knew so well, now full of

73

colorful leather spines, framing the same stone alcove. The lush velvet curtains to the alcove were closed, but the room was unmistakable. "Oh my goblin! You're right!"

"You're *almost* right," came Zarya's voice. Her head appeared above the railing that separated the landing from the fountain, followed a second later by Piper's.

"Aaaah, you're here!" Piper burst out. "You have to come and see this! Come come comecomecomecome!" She waggled her hands at them insistently.

Em, Arkayna, and Doug ran up the flight of stairs onto the landing and joined Zarya and Piper. "Why didn't you say something as soon as we arrived?" asked Arkayna as they approached.

"We didn't notice you until you started talking," said Zarya. "The fountain was in the way, and besides, we were a little distracted by, uh . . ." She motioned out the window.

Em glanced through the stained glass, expecting to see the usual view of packed dirt, stone, and rubble. The Stronghold, after all, was built two castles and as many earthquakes ago, and it had been buried underground for

hundreds of— Then her eyes focused. All thought went out of her head and she froze, staring.

"Well, I'll be a kobold's cousin," breathed Doug.

They were aboveground. That was the first thing Em's overloaded brain was able to process. High aboveground. The sun was shining down on a wide plaza flanked by colorful banners. Around and past the plaza were the rooftops of a crowded city. It looked like the royal plaza in Drake City, and this view of the city *kind of* looked like the palace district. Except . . . Em shook her head. She was still missing something. Crouching down, she leaned into the huge window and peered closer. Figures moved through the plaza on various business—a phalanx of soldiers marched, a couple strolled arm in arm, a vendor pushed a wooden cart. . . . The cart was what did it.

"Cars!" Em said. "There are no cars." She looked out over the city. "And there's no dragon train." She squinted down at the plaza again. "Those lights along the boulevard are torches; it's like no one's even *heard* of hexpowered . . ." Her words died as she struggled to take it all in.

"This is the castle," Arkayna whispered next to her. Then, louder, as she gained confidence, "This is *the* castle. I know where we are." She took a deep breath and let it out slowly. "We're in Drake City. A thousand years ago."

The dramatic silence after her pronouncement was broken by Piper saying, "Well, *duh.*"

In Which Things Heat Up

10

"THIS WHOLE THING IS THE SECOND PUZZLE," ZARYA WAS explaining as they made their way down to street level. "We didn't actually go back in time or anything; this is just a simulation. It's a big game, or a riddle. There must be something for us to do, a quest or something, and when we do it the puzzle is solved!"

A servant in fancy clothes approached, going the other direction on the stairs. Catching sight of the group, he stopped and bowed deferentially, waiting for them to pass. Em side-eyed him warily as she responded to Zarya.

"A . . . big game? But who are all these other people? Who's *this*?"

"He's probably no one," answered Zarya. The servant raised his head and arched his eyebrows in surprise. "Sorry," Zarya told him, "I don't mean *no one*. I just mean, you're part of the puzzle, right? Are you a questgiver?"

The servant straightened and looked confused. "I'm afraid I don't know what you mean, Sir Ranger. Am I a *what*?"

"Oh," Zarya sighed, "right. You're all in character."

"This is so cool!" Doug chimed in. "It's just like *Remembered Realms*! Let me try." He turned to face the flabbergasted servant. "Are you . . . uh . . . having any problems around here today?"

"Of course not, sir," the servant replied. He smiled, relieved to be back on familiar ground, and motioned at the girls. "The Mysticons are here to keep Drake City safe from harm."

"Oh, sure, the Mysticons are great," Doug said, playing along and nodding. "But, still—is there something we can help with? Maybe you need something delivered? Or you lost something?"

The servant shifted from foot to foot, confused again. "Um. No, sir. But even if I did, I would not trouble the Mysticons with my trifles."

Zarya leaned toward Doug and stage-whispered, "It's not him." Then she addressed the servant in an over-blown, old-fashioned accent: "Thank you, noble sir. You've been most gracious to us this fine day."

Backing up the stairs, looking even more uncomfort-able, the servant replied, "You're very kind, Sir Ranger." Then he bowed his head to Em, Piper, and Arkayna in turn, saying, "Sir Knight. Madam Striker. Madam Dragon Mage." Last, he turned to Doug and faltered. "Sir . . . uh, sir." He turned and hustled away, leaving the group to stare at each other in bemusement.

Arkayna turned to Zarya and Em. "He called you both 'sir.' He thinks we're the original Mysticons!"

"Well, sure," said Em, "that's who these puzzles were built for, right?"

"But he didn't know *what* to do with Doug," Piper giggled.

Before Doug could react, Em jumped in: "Because Doug isn't officially the fifth Mysticon yet! But he *is* an important part of the team already. Without him, Arkayna and I could have gotten cooked by a unicorn just now, right, Arkayna?"

"Right," Arkayna said distractedly. She started down the stairs again. "I guess we'd better go find this quest, then!"

"Cooked by a . . . what?" Zarya asked, following. "We were only split up for a minute!"

A little while later, they were even more confused. None of the passersby or guards seemed to need anything. The city seemed peaceful and pleasantly busy. Soon they had wandered all the way to Magi Mall, which in this ancient version of Drake City was an open-air market in a large square plaza. Vendors hawked their wares from shaded carts and tapestry-draped kiosks. Musicians played from a small raised stage in the middle of the square.

"Hey, remember? We saw a map of this place, when we were looking for my Codex piece!" said Piper. "And we found it in the ruins of the old temple underneath the mall. Maybe we should go to the temple!"

"It's as good an idea as any," sighed Zarya. They headed through the crowded plaza toward the temple.

"I wish we knew what we're supposed to do!" complained Arkayna. "Like, if there were something that needed doing in *our* Drake City, we could find it by watching the news, or look it up on our bangle-phones, or someone would just glyph us about it!"

"And I don't want to whine," put in Em, "but walking all over the city is *very* slow. I miss the dragon train. And our griffins! Oh, do I miss our griffins."

Zarya held up her hands to ward off a particularly pushy vendor, who was following her with a glowing vial in each hand and would not stop talking. "No, I don't need a miracle cure, thank you," she told him. "Or a love potion. No, really. No, *really*."

Finally the merchant got the point and, shoulders drooping, turned back to his stall. "Ugh," Zarya continued in a more muttered tone, " 'charm the special man in your life.' No, thank you."

"I don't know," said Doug, looking around, "I still think this is pretty cool."

"*Pff*," Piper scoffed, "try living without your bangle-phone for more than a few days, *then* tell me it's cool. But you won't"—she poked him in the side for emphasis—"because it. Is. Not. I remember what life was like before bangle-phones, and I do *not* want to go back there, thank you very much. Now let's go find—"

A strange coughing sound came from above them, and then: *BWOOM!* The potion kiosk behind them exploded into flames. The merchant, still returning from harrying Zarya, was thrown flat on his back by the blast. A split second later, as screams erupted throughout the marketplace, the intense heat wave washed over the Mysticons and Doug, making them flinch.

"What in the . . ." Em looked around for the source of the fireball and drew in a sharp breath. "Well, good news, everyone!" she said in a forced, cheery tone. "I found our quest."

The sky was full of monsters.

In Which There Are Several Types of Bad Breath

11

EM QUICKLY COUNTED THEM OFF IN HER HEAD: *ONE TWO THREE four five SIX.* Six rocs, huge birds ten times the size of a griffin, were descending on the city in a *V* formation. The one in the lead, lava dripping from its beak, was deep red. The others in the *V* were green, white, blue, and purple. And bringing up the rear, largest of all, was a huge black roc, its beak parted in what Em could swear was a grin.

"All right!" Zarya shouted, leaping on top of a nearby fruit cart for a better vantage point. *"Boss fight!"* She nocked an arrow, took aim at the crimson roc, and fired.

To her surprise, the arrow bounced right off its beak. The huge beast didn't even flinch.

"I call the green one!" said Piper, somersaulting through the air and tossing her hoops at her target. The emerald roc didn't bother to dodge. It swatted the hoops out of the air with its giant wings, then dropped into a dive.

"Okay, let's try something with a little more *oomph*," Em called, pulling three orbs out of her pouch. "Heads up!" As the green roc swooped over their heads, she hurled the orbs up at its exposed belly. They beeped twice, then exploded in a cloud of smoke with a *fwa-BOOM* that Em felt in her gut.

But when the smoke cleared, Em cried out in disappointment. The roc was completely unharmed. Its feathers weren't even singed. Opening its beak wide, it exhaled a cloud of green gas at a family of terrified elves.

Arkayna was just in time. She fired her staff at the elves, and a dome of energy sprung into place around them as the roc's gas descended. The family sagged in relief as the noxious fumes wafted harmlessly around the protective dome, dispersing in the air.

"Something's wrong!" Zarya shouted desperately.

"Why can't we hurt them?" She drew and fired, drew and fired at each roc in turn. And one by one—red roc, green, white, blue, purple—the arrows bounced and fizzled off, to no effect. Zarya fired one last arrow at the faraway black roc, who backed up leisurely to hover in place. The arrow fell short, and the beast snorted in amusement.

The blue roc swooped down, spitting jagged shards of ice from its beak as it came. People dove for cover as the razor-sharp icicles fell from the sky, impaling kiosks and driving themselves deep into the stone ground with the force of their impacts. Narrowing its eyes, the huge bird made a beeline for Zarya, still standing atop the cart.

"Uh, so, don't worry," Zarya stammered. "This is all part of the game. It probably can't hurt me. Probably." Her hands shaking slightly, she nocked and aimed another arrow. "Maybe the trick is to wait until it's closer?" As the roc bore down on her, she waited three seconds . . . four seconds . . . *five*. She fired.

The roc snapped its beak and plucked the arrow from the air effortlessly, breaking it in two.

"Nope!" cried Zarya. She looked around for a hiding place, but the roc was almost on top of her. It drew in breath to fire. At this range, there was no way the ice would miss.

"Aaaa*aaaaaah*!" Suddenly Doug came charging into the open. Bending down, he grabbed an apple from the spilled cart and, in a last-ditch attempt to distract the roc, chucked the fruit right at its huge head.

Em watched hopelessly as the apple arced through the air and impacted one blue feathered cheek with an almost inaudible *bop*. But the roc reared back in surprise, veering off course and smashing through a line of nearby kiosks. It choked on its ice attack and went into what seemed to be a coughing fit. Hacking in alarm, it careened through the square and crashed into the empty bandstand in the center.

Doug looked down at the apples, then up at the Mysticons. "It's . . . allergic?" he guessed.

Jumping down off the cart, Zarya grabbed a stick of wood from the nearest broken stand. "I bet they can only be hurt by things from *inside* the puzzle."

"Got it!" Piper ran over to a smashed barrel and pried three hoops free from the wood. "You are my new Hoopys," she told the slightly misshapen bits of metal. "Make me proud." She ran into a clear space and scanned the sky. "Who's next? Lemme at 'em!"

Holding her stick, Zarya ran out to stand back-to-back with Piper, while Doug gathered up all the apples he could hold. Arkayna started to join them, but hesitated. She glanced at the sky, then at the chaotic marketplace. All around them, people were running for the cover of buildings, or cowering underneath whatever they could find out in the square.

Zarya caught her look. "We'll draw their fire," she yelled to Arkayna. "You and Em have the shields."

Arkayna nodded resolutely. "We'll get everyone out of here safely." She turned to Em. "Let's do this!"

As she spoke, the white roc, circling overhead, caught sight of Zarya and Piper. It wheeled around and plunged toward them.

"Here we go," muttered Zarya, and she threw her stick like a spear. The wood parted the crest of upright feathers on the roc's head, but had no other effect.

"Go! Go! Go!" Piper shouted after her hoops as she

threw them. The roc lifted its head, and the first two hoops bounced off its neck. The third caught on one of its crest feathers and hung there, like an earring.

"Bugbears," muttered Zarya. "What are we doing wrong?"

Rumbling low in its throat, the white roc opened its jaws and spat. A translucent glob flew out of its mouth and splatted over Zarya and Piper, coating them from head to toe.

"Uch!" Piper squealed. "Bird spit!" She reached up to wipe the goo out of her hair, and then froze as her right hand wouldn't come away from her head. "Sticky bird spit!" She braced her left hand against her other wrist and, pulling as hard as she could, managed to get her right hand free.

"Oh no," Zarya said. "It's all over our feet. We have to move before it dries, or we'll be stuck here!"

"Coming!" shouted Doug. He sprinted over to them, apples spilling from his pockets, and bent down to begin yanking at Zarya's legs.

"RrrrrRRRR!" Piper tried her hardest to run, but it was like wading through molasses. "What kind of roc spits glue?" She shook her sticky fists at the sky. "You are not a fun game, birdie!"

Roaring in triumph, the white roc beat its wings and soared back into the air. Its red counterpart, sensing trapped prey, began to descend while making a coughing sound deep in its throat.

"Is that the one . . ." began Doug.

"That hacks up fireballs, yeah," Zarya finished. "We gotta go!"

Meanwhile, Arkayna and Em were racing for the center of the square, where several people were sheltering in flimsy kiosks or underneath upturned wagons. They were all too scared to move, and the blue roc, pulling itself up from the wreckage of the bandstand, was going to notice them at any second. But as Arkayna and Em ran, the purple roc streaked down and thudded to the ground in front of the blue. It lowered its head to ground level and stretched its beak wide.

The two girls skidded to a halt. Arkayna held up her staff and Em put a hand to her pouch, preparing to counter whatever was about to come out of the purple roc's mouth.

But nothing came out. Instead, the roc sucked in a huge breath . . . and kept inhaling. A sudden wind ripped through the plaza, blowing the coverings off of kiosks and causing loose bits of wood and debris to skate several feet toward the bandstand. The roc inhaled again, and Em heard a squeal and a shout of "Beryl!" Just to her left was a dwarven family sheltering in a pottery kiosk. The family's little girl—Em assumed her name was Beryl— had lost her grip on her mother and was skidding, out of control, directly toward the vacuum of the roc's mouth.

Arkayna began firing energy blasts from her staff at the roc, but they fizzled against its purple feathers.

"Doug!" That was Zarya's voice. Em risked a glance behind her to see the crimson roc descending on Piper, Zarya, and Doug.

"Help!" Beryl was halfway to the purple roc now, frantically scrabbling at the ground to slow herself.

Em began to panic. Maybe she had been wrong all along. Maybe this wasn't a puzzle. Maybe this was just a trap!

In Which Several Things Prove
Mightier Than Swords

12

"DOUG!" ZARYA YELLED. "YOUR APPLES! QUICK!"

"Oh, man," said Doug, straightening and reaching into a pocket. "Okay, if you say so!" He took aim and threw an apple at the approaching crimson roc.

Bap! The apple hit right between its eyes. The roc shrieked, and Doug threw again. This one hit the inside of its mouth, and its eyes widened in shock.

"Again!" Piper clapped her hands, then grunted in annoyance as they stuck together.

Doug continued to pelt the roc with apples, making

it hiss in confusion, while Zarya and Piper worked to free themselves.

Back by the bandstand, Em pulled herself together. Trap or not, she told herself, puzzle or not, she was going to save all these people. Even if they were imaginary. "Armor out!" she shouted, tossing an orb at her feet. Her mech suit expanded around her, and she dashed toward the girl. Inches from the purple roc's lolling tongue, Em snatched Beryl up and began pounding back toward Arkayna, the heavy suit protecting her from its suction breath. "Our offense doesn't work!" she called. "Try defense!"

Arkayna nodded and fired again. This time a huge dome settled into place over the blue and purple rocs. The wind howling across the plaza cut off abruptly, just as Em reached Beryl's family and handed her over.

"Oh, thank the stars," said the father. "We thought she was—"

FWAM! CRACK! The two trapped rocs threw themselves against Arkayna's forcefield, smashing it to pieces. The blue began to beat its wings, preparing to take off, while the purple opened its mouth again.

"Not this time!" cried Beryl's mother. She picked up a pottery jug and hurled it at the purple. The jug smashed against the roc's sharp beak, and the shards of pottery flew down its throat. It screeched in pain and began to wheeze.

"That's right!" bellowed Beryl's father. "And *you*!" He hefted a heavy mug in his hands, testing its weight, and then flung it at the blue. His aim was good, and the mug caught the roc in the chest. The blue squawked in protest, its wings faltering. Emboldened, the father charged forward. "Come on!" he said, beckoning to another couple sheltering under a wagon. "We can do this!"

Em looked at Arkayna in surprise as Zarya, Piper, and Doug came pounding up behind them. "We drove the red off for now," Zarya panted. "Well, Doug did."

"Doug's the only one who can hurt them," Piper added. "He's got the magic apples."

"And I'm almost out!" said Doug mournfully.

"It's not the apples," Em realized. "And you're not the only one who can hurt them." She looked around at the other girls. "We're the only ones who *can't*."

"But, but," Zarya protested, pointing at the people

starting to mobilize against the rocs, "they're going to get themselves killed!"

"You're right," said Arkayna. "They need our help. But *they* have to do the actual attacking."

"Awwww," complained Piper. "I wanna hit the monsters!"

"Arkayna's right," Em said. "This is about inspiring people, not doing everything ourselves." She glanced over and noticed a few of the braver folks, Beryl's mother and two merchants, advancing on the rocs in a line. "Wait, hold on!" she yelled, charging after them in her mech suit. "You've gotta use cover if you're gonna do that!"

Zarya beckoned to a group of people huddled behind a stall of paintings. "Hey, everyone," she said. "Let's go over this way; we can get a good flank on them." She took her group in a wide circle around the bandstand, darting from kiosk to kiosk.

Beryl's father looked around for something else to throw. Noticing a cart full of rolled-up rugs, the dwarf grabbed one and started whipping it back and forth through the air like a club. He grunted in satisfaction, propped the rug on his shoulder, and faced the rocs again.

"Wait!" Doug ran up behind him and put a hand on his shoulder. The dwarf spun, raising the rug threateningly. "No no," Doug hastened to say, "we're cool, man. I just want to give you this." He held out a gray potion. "You looked like you wanted to charge right in there, so here. It's Stone Skin. It'll make you tougher and heavier, which"—he motioned to the blue and purple rocs, who were both readying to attack—"you know."

The father nodded his thanks, then downed the potion. His grimace at the taste soon stretched into a grin as his skin crackled and hardened. He stamped the ground, and the flagstone under his foot split in two. "Ha!" he barked. Still chuckling grimly, he hefted his makeshift weapon and charged into battle.

The purple roc started to open its mouth, but it never had a chance. Swinging the rug wildly from side to side, Beryl's father leaped and smashed the roc right in the face, then in the gut, then in the leg. The beast squealed in dismay under the onslaught, scrambling backward until it bumped into the blue roc. It looked over at the blue frantically and shook its head once. Then it flapped its huge wings and took off, wheeling until it was no longer in view.

A cheer went up from the square. But it was quickly drowned out by a roar as the white roc landed in the purple's place. There were more monsters yet to beat!

Piper and Doug joined another group of people behind a baker's stall. "Okay," Piper told them, "these things seem to *hate* food. But you gotta aim for the squishy parts. Eyes, belly, inside the mouth, like that. Okay?"

Doug turned to one teenage human, who was staring out at the rocs, eyes wide, holding a slingshot in her hands. "Hi. I'm Doug. You any good with that?" he asked.

She looked down at the slingshot, then back up at Doug. "My name's Sylvie. I use this at home to keep the birds off the wheat," she said. "But . . ."

"Don't worry," said Doug, "I can help." He handed her a bright green potion. "This is True Aim. Whatever you shoot, it'll go where it's supposed to."

"Really?" At Doug's nod, she drank the potion. A new sparkle seemed to come to her eyes, and she whispered, "Wow. Oh, wow. I can see *everything.*"

Doug handed her a biscuit. "Show me."

Quickly, Sylvie loaded the biscuit into the slingshot and stood up from cover. The white roc looked right at her, and she froze.

"Squishies," said Piper encouragingly. "You got this."

Sylvie drew back the slingshot and fired. Like an arrow, the biscuit streaked across the square and hit— *thunk*—squarely in the middle of the white roc's staring eye. The roc roared in pain.

"See?" cheered Piper. "Squishies every time."

Arkayna saw the white roc was distracted and called, "Em, now!"

Em motioned her group forward, and Beryl's mother and the two merchants ran out and stabbed at the white roc with makeshift spears. The blue looked over and, seeing what was happening, opened its beak to attack.

"Zarya!" shouted Arkayna.

A barrage of sticks and rubble arced toward the blue from the bandstand, where Zarya and her group had been hiding. The blue roc was pelted from behind and screamed in frustration. Together, the blue and white rocs took off and flapped away hastily.

"Three down!" Arkayna looked up at the sky, where the red and green rocs were forming up to dive. But seeing what happened to their friends, they thought better of their plan. Instead of attacking, they turned and fled. Arkayna laughed, "Make that five!"

But the battle wasn't over yet. With a series of huge wingflaps, the giant black roc descended into the marketplace. It landed with a *thud*, tipped back its head, and let out a deafening screech. The force of the shout made everyone clap their hands to their ears.

And then the fear hit. It seemed to roll over them in a wave. Em started to sweat and felt her hands shaking. She tried to turn her head toward the roc and had to fight away her terror just to look at it. What was it about this roc? And then she realized, "This is magic! It's a fear spell!" She looked around the square and saw everyone cowering helplessly. "It's just a spell!" she shouted again. But, still, her voice quaked.

Em saw Arkayna take a deep breath, force herself to stand up straight, and open her mouth. But nothing came out. Arkayna cleared her throat and tried again. "I-is—"

"Arkayna!" Em called. "Look at us instead of the roc!"

Arkayna locked eyes with Em and smiled. "Is this bird serious?" she asked, her voice steadier. "You fought off beasts that spit fire! And ice! And poison! And now this thing thinks it can just *scare* you?" She jumped up on the nearest cart. "Fear is all this monster's got!" she shouted, totally sure of herself now. She looked out over the square, making eye contact with Zarya, then Piper, then Doug, who all smiled up at her proudly. She grinned wildly and pointed at the crowd with her staff. *"Let's show it what WE'VE got!"*

With a roar, the people surged forward to attack. The roc shrieked again, this time in fear itself. And as it did, everything went white.

*In Which a Lock Opens
and a Trap Closes*

13

WHEN EM'S VISION BEGAN TO CLEAR, SHE SAW THAT THEY were back in the Chillwaste. The mist that had swallowed them was rising up into the air, leaving them crouched in various positions around the chasm—except for Arkayna, who was striking a heroic pose astride a low rock. As they watched, the mist flew upward to the group of stars above. It seemed to cling to some of the stars and obscure them, making them fade back into the black night sky. The remaining stars were now clustered in a rough, long rectangle.

Piper craned her neck and tipped her head from side to side, trying to make sense of the stars that were left. "Is it . . . a snake?" she asked. "Maybe a sword?"

"I don't think we're supposed to know yet," said Em. "It'll probably get clearer after we deal with the next puzzle."

"Oh, yeah, show us this unicorn!" Zarya said. "That sounded cool."

"Sure, cool," said Em. "And deadly. Cool and deadly. This way."

As they began to retrace their steps to the ice sculpture of the original Mysticons, Arkayna put her hand on Doug's shoulder. "That was nice work back there, with the rocs."

Doug shrugged. "I didn't really do that much."

"What?!" cried Piper, leaping in front of him. She walked backward, looking up at him while ticking points off on her fingers. "You drove off the big red guy, *and* made that little girl's father unstoppable, *and* made that girl Sylvie into a crack-shot sniper person, *and* you never panicked, not even once! I was counting!" She faced front again, just in time to avoid colliding with the ice sculpture. "Eep!"

"Piper's right," added Zarya. "You really stepped up. Everyone did." She sighed. "I wasn't really into the part where we had to put other people at risk, though."

"I think it was more than that," Em put in thoughtfully. "We weren't just hanging back and letting them do the work for us." She motioned to Zarya and Piper. "Each group needed different advice from us to make their attacks work." She pointed to Arkayna. "And we all needed someone to coordinate us. If we hadn't been willing to stay in the background, doing those things, the rocs would have won."

"It was about doing what needed to be done instead of going for the glory," Arkayna mused as they turned down the right-hand path, "and the first puzzle was about looking past the shiniest, most tempting thing."

"For a bunch of cursed locks," Piper said, "these sure are teaching us some heroic stuff."

"Huh," said Zarya, "that's a good point."

"It is, it really is," said Arkayna. "I feel like we're missing some—"

"Careful!" Doug cut her off. "Zappy unicorn is waking up!"

Em looked up at the unicorn looming out of the left-hand wall. Sure enough, its horn was starting to glow red again. With a grinding rumble, it slowly raised its gigantic head.

Just past the unicorn, the path took a sharp turn to the right. And on the far wall, facing Doug and the Mysticons, a huge wolf statue crouched, half-in and half-out of the stone. The claws on its front paw, each the size of Em, raked the ground as the wolf bared its teeth, exposing a shiny blue gem it held in its jaws.

"Go!" called Em. "I'll cover you!"

Arkayna, Zarya, Piper, and Doug darted past Em and down the path, dodging the wolf's paws as they crashed to the ground again. The unicorn's horn fired its laser, and Em summoned her shield and braced herself. Still, she was shoved back as the laser connected. The unicorn tossed its head from side to side, firing its horn in short bursts. With each blast, Em was pushed toward the wolf's sharp claws. She corrected her stance, but the impacts kept coming. Now her feet were sliding away from the wolf, but she was being forced toward the sharp corner where the path turned. Glancing behind her, she saw the corner was made of smooth, unbroken stone.

"Better than that wolf's stompy feet," she muttered to herself, and she allowed the laser blasts to push her until her back leg connected with the wall.

Abruptly, the unicorn's horn stopped firing. Em took a breath, dropping her shield. But before she could look down the path for her friends, two hands made of stone erupted from the wall behind her, grabbing her and pinning her arms to her sides. She couldn't move!

In Which Practice Makes Perfect,
and Red, Blue, and Green Make White

14

EM LOOKED TO HER RIGHT. DOUG, ARKAYNA, PIPER, AND ZARYA were safe at the end of the short path, staring up at the walls around them. Farther down the same wall as Em, a huge phoenix erupted from the stone, dangling one large green jewel from its beak and two more from its claws. Along the wall opposite her, a gargantuan stone tail snaked toward the end of the path, where it joined with a towering dragon. The dragon held its front legs stiffly out in front of it. Its eyes, tipped up to the sky, were two white gems.

"Little help here?" Em called to her friends.

With cries of alarm, everyone came rushing toward her. As they approached, the unicorn stomped the ground and lowered its glowing horn. Arkayna threw up a dome around the five of them just in time. Shattering the force-field, the unicorn's laser deflected into several smaller beams ricocheting in all directions. One beam hit the blue gem in the wolf's mouth and bounced off, turning magenta as it blasted back down the path toward the ice statue of the original Mysticons.

"Ohhhhhh," said Em, "I think I know what the gems are for."

"Let's worry about that in a minute, okay?" Arkayna said, throwing up another dome. "Everybody pull!"

While Arkayna renewed the shield around them after each laser blast, Zarya, Piper, and Doug pulled at the stone arms holding Em captive. But no matter how hard they strained and tugged, Em was held fast.

"Doug, do you have anything in your potion belt that's acidic enough to melt stone?" asked Arkayna.

"Uh, I don't think so," replied Doug. He peered at his phone, scrolling through the list Malvaron had made him.

"These are all for drinking, not melting. Oh, and for future reference, apparently True Aim tastes best poured over cereal. Huh."

"Em, we can't blast you out without hurting you," Arkayna said, "and you can't get your mech suit on while you're stuck in there. I don't know how we—"

"I do," said Em. "You solve this one without me."

"But *you* said we all needed to open the locks together," protested Arkayna.

"That's true," Em said. "But whoever designed this puzzle didn't know there would be five of us. Doug can take my place!"

"I can what now?" said Doug.

"Take your place doing what?" asked Zarya. "We don't even know what this puzzle is about yet."

"Yes, we do," Em said. "We need to bounce the beam from the unicorn's horn off all these gems. See how the one in the wolf's mouth points back along the path? It needs to point over there instead." She jerked her head toward the phoenix.

"Well, that's easy enough," said Zarya.

The next time Arkayna's shield went down, Zarya

fired an arrow at the gem in the wolf's mouth. It was a perfect shot, glancing off the far right side of the faceted jewel. The blue gem creaked as it rotated to face the phoenix . . . and then kept rotating, all the way back to its original position.

"Hmmmm," said Em. "So it's a timing puzzle, too."

Another blast hit Arkayna's shield, and again a dozen reflected lasers bounced off the high chasm walls as the shield shattered. There were now hundreds of scorch marks up and down the pathway.

"Using this dome can't be right," Arkayna said. "I need to be more precise. I wonder if . . ." Instead of throwing another shield up, she stepped forward on the path and held her staff at the ready.

This time, when the laser came, Arkayna thrust the staff into the air so that its orb caught the blast. Arkayna's arm was thrown backward from the force of the beam, and the laser reflected back directly at the unicorn, which bared its teeth in challenge.

"Ow!" Arkayna shook out her arms and reset her stance. "Okay, I can do better. Let me try again."

When the next blast came, she swung the staff like a

bat. This time, the orb caught the blast and deflected it up toward the wolf, sizzling into the space right between its eyes. The wolf wrinkled its muzzle and snarled angrily.

"I'm getting it." Arkayna squared her shoulders in determination. "I'll keep trying."

"I found my job!" called Piper happily. Perched on the last loop of the dragon's tail, she faced the phoenix across the path. "Lookie look!" She summoned three hoops into her hand and threw them all at once. The hoops arced through the air, hitting the phoenix's three green gems and setting them spinning. As they turned, Em saw what she had missed at first glance: One side of each gem was scratched, pitted, and dull. Piper would have to time her throws exactly to make the laser bounce from gem to gem across the shiny sides.

"Okay," Em muttered, "and then the beam goes to . . . where? The dragon's eyes?"

"All the way at the top?" asked Doug, overhearing her. "That looks tough. Hold on, I'll go look." He jogged the length of the path, and as he approached the dragon he called back over his shoulder. "Nope! It's the palms! There are clear gems in the palms!"

"Do they spin?" shouted Em.

"No, they're just stuck in there," Doug yelled back. He went to stand under one of the huge dragon's forelegs, peering up at its downturned foot. "But if Piper gets the beam aimed at . . . well, at me, I could try to bounce it up. With . . . some . . . thing?"

Arkayna glanced back at Em after batting away another laser. "I bet this is where your shield would come in, Em."

"Yeah, but we don't have that," Em said, "so let's figure out what we do have. Hey, Doug! We need something sturdy and reflective; what have you got?"

"I am so glad you asked!" said Doug happily. He shrugged off his oversized backpack and began unpacking its contents on the ground in front of the gigantic dragon. "I have a pot. . . . It's not very shiny, though. This silverware is shiny, but it's so small. . . ."

As he continued rummaging, Arkayna deflected another laser with her staff. This one hit the wolf's gem squarely in the center. "Yesssssss!" She celebrated with a quick fist pump. "Zarya, Piper, I'm ready here. How are you?"

"Born ready," said Zarya. She nocked an arrow and aimed steadily at the wolf.

"Ready Freddie!" chirped Piper, summoning three more hoops to her hands.

"Doug?" called Arkayna.

From the end of the path, Doug heaved a small, defeated sigh.

"Doug? You okay?" Em asked.

"Yeah," Doug replied. "I found something that will work."

"That's great!" said Arkayna. "Get it ready!"

"Well, I mean . . . okay." Doug turned around and raised his hand. In it, he held the hard, sparkly figure of Glimmer Gust.

"Uh," Zarya said after a pause, "is that gonna work?"

"It *is* made of limited-edition crystal," said Em sadly. "Oh, Doug."

"It's okay," Doug replied, one corner of his mouth pulling up in a smile. "There are a hundred and ninety-nine more of them, right?"

"Let's get this done," declared Arkayna.

When the next laser came, Arkayna swung her staff

hard and deflected the red blast into the wolf's mouth. As she did, Zarya loosed her arrow, and the blue gem caught the beam and fired it, magenta now, directly at the phoenix's foot.

"Woo-hooooo!" shouted Piper, tossing her hoops. She set the phoenix's jewels spinning with a series of *clang*s. As the phoenix's stone feathers ruffled in an invisible breeze, the magenta beam bounced between the three green gems and emerged, now a white blast that was pointed directly at Doug.

Doug grimaced and held the Twinkly Mare out in front of him, angling it up toward the dragon's foot and bracing it with his other hand. The white blast hit the toy and reflected off, shooting upward. The clear gem absorbed the beam, and Em saw the dragon's eyes glitter briefly. But then . . . nothing.

The unicorn fired another blast, almost taking the stunned Arkayna by surprise. She managed to bat it away at the last possible moment, then turned to Em. "What are we missing?" she asked, wild-eyed.

Em shook her head. She had no idea.

In Which a Captor
and a Captive Are Revealed

15

"THIS IS SO FRUSTRATING!" EM CRIED. "YOU'RE ALL OUT
there putting yourselves in the path of deadly lasers, and
I'm stuck here in *this* thing."

Piper came over and patted her consolingly on the
head. "At least it's a cute thing."

"It's a . . . it's a what?" It had never occurred to Em that
the arms holding her might be attached to a creature. She
craned her neck back, but all she could see above her was
some sort of chin and maybe . . . were those wings?
"What's got me?"

"Oh, just the most adorable little foz!" said Piper. "Well, it's actually pretty huge, and it does have a kind of grumpy look on its face. But that just makes it cuter! I'd pinch its cheeks if they weren't made of stone!"

"I'd shoot it right in the ear if it weren't made of stone!" complained Zarya. "I might do it anyway. We need our Knight in the fight!"

"Ah, those are ears. Not wings. Wait." Em looked at Arkayna, who was standing right next to her, continuing to bat lasers away as they came streaking out of the unicorn's horn. "I know what we're missing!"

"*Please* tell me," said Arkayna. "My arms are starting to get tired."

"We're not thinking enough like the original Mysticons," said Em. "First of all, the original Knight didn't use a shield, he had a big old sword instead. Second, the original Dragon Mage would never, ever want to be where you are, Arkayna. She was afraid of foz."

"So you're saying . . ." Arkayna tried to think it through but was distracted by another blast from the unicorn.

"You and Doug need to switch places!" cried Em.

"Doug can be here and swing the Twinkly Mare like the original Knight would have swung his sword. And you can go stand down there—far, far away from this foz— and split the beam into two parts with your staff! That way you hit both of the dragon gems at one time!"

"It's worth a try," said Arkayna. "Doug?"

"Coming!" Doug trotted up to stand next to Arkayna as Piper and Zarya took their places again. "Any tips for me?"

"Plant your feet," Arkayna said. "It packs a wallop."

"Okay." He looked down at Glimmer Gust, now scorched black all along one side. Digging his back foot into the ground, Doug faced the unicorn and held the still-shiny side of the toy up toward the horn. "I hope this works," he said, "because I think we only get one more shot."

"You can do this, Doug!" Em cheered. "You're one of us!"

Fwoom! The unicorn fired.

"Oof!" Doug let out his breath in a rush as the blast hit the Twinkly Mare. He pivoted, twisting his body to send the beam flying at the wolf.

Spang! Zarya's arrow hit the blue gem at the same time as the beam, which changed color and ricocheted toward the phoenix.

Ting! Tang! Clang! Piper's hoops found their marks, and the magenta beam found its way through the spinning green gems, turning white on the way, and headed for where Arkayna stood, under and between the dragon's outstretched paws. She held up her staff.

Fzzzzzzzzt! The shining white blast hit the staff's orb dead-on, crackling as it split in two and bounced up into the dragon's clear gems.

This time, the dragon's eyes glowed a brilliant white. Beams of pure energy shot out of both eyes, aimed at either side of the constellation overhead. The energy seemed to pour into the outermost stars and then shot to the nearby stars, connecting them in points, loops, and whorls all along the formation. As the giant foz released Em and retreated into the wall, the dragon's eyes dimmed, and the beam went out, leaving all the stars connected to spell an unmistakable word.

"'Rogue'?" wondered Arkayna.

"*YESSSSSSSSSSS!*" came the voice of the fifth Mysticon. "*AT LAST!*"

The stars and light began to swirl and twist, contracting on themselves and re-forming into a tiny humanoid outline. The outline sharpened, resolving from a white glow into hard edges. Then it began to grow.

"Wait, wasn't this prison supposed to be holding the fifth Mysticon's spirit?" asked Zarya.

"Yeeeees," said Em, hesitating.

"Well, I've got news for you. That's not a spirit. That's a *person*. And it's falling out of the sky!"

In Which Toes Are Stepped On,
and a Heel Is Turned

16

EM GRABBED AT HER HAIR IN DISTRESS. "HOW DO WE CATCH her? Doug, grab that blanket from your pack. Maybe if we stretch it—"

"No need, Knight," the voice hissed triumphantly. "No need at all."

A moment later, the falling figure was close enough for Em to see that it was a dwarven girl in tattered clothes. A moment after that, the girl's eyes flew open and flared gold, and she grinned.

Piper started to babble, "She's gonna hit the horn she's

gonna hit the horn and the horn looks very very very stabby, she's gonna—"

The second before the unicorn's horn would have impaled her, the girl twisted in midair and tucked her legs underneath her. She pushed off the side of the horn at an angle, her momentum carrying her toward the wolf's mouth. Reaching up to grab the ridge of its lower teeth, she swung underneath the wolf's chin, sprung off the wall next to its neck, and somersaulted across the path over them to land neatly on the phoenix's head. Then she used the ridge of the phoenix's wing like a giant slide, skidding down its shoulder and catapulting off the upturned wing-tip, before turning one more flip in midair and landing nimbly on the ground in front of them. Still grinning, she sketched a bow.

"You have my thanks, Mysticons." Here she looked to Doug, standing slack-jawed, still clutching the scorched Twinkly Mare in his hands. She cocked an eyebrow. "And Doug, for reuniting my spirit and my long-imprisoned body."

Doug realized he was staring and closed his mouth with an audible *click*, ducking his head in embarrassment.

Arkayna stepped forward to cover his awkwardness. "You're welcome. In return, it's time for you to finally answer our questions. Let's start with: Who are you?"

"I," the girl announced, "am Mysticon Rogue!" As she spoke, a wave of power shimmered over her body and transformed her clothes. A gold headpiece stretched down either side of her face, its tendrils touching the corners of her eyes and curling around behind her ears. A black full-body suit with gold accents replaced her tattered shirt and pants, high black boots covered her bare feet, and gold daggers flickering with black flames appeared in her hands.

Zarya spoke up. "So, do we just call you 'Rogue'?"

"That will do for now, yes," replied the Rogue, sheathing her daggers. "There will be time for more stories once we're out of this place. Come." She strode up the path, back toward the ice sculpture. As the others followed, stammering questions, she continued. "For now it is enough to know that I am the master of stealth. I show up where my enemies least expect. I can disarm any trap, and I can get past any lock."

Behind her, Em watched as Arkayna frowned, Doug

tried for a polite smile that turned into a grimace, and Piper and Zarya rolled their eyes at each other. This fifth Mysticon was not making a great first impression. Piper said, "Not any lock. We had to come let you out!"

The Rogue stopped short and hissed in irritation. Then she seemed to catch herself and spun to face them. "But you came," she replied. She rocked forward on her toes, leaning uncomfortably close to Piper. "Not all lock-picks are made of metal, little elf girl."

"Whoa now," said Zarya, her eyes widening in disbelief.

"Who're you calling little?" demanded Piper, stretching up on tiptoes.

Em raised her voice as she stepped between Piper and the Rogue, arms out to keep them apart. "Okay!" She faced the Rogue. "Generally I go way out of my way to avoid being rude to people I have just met, but you are pushing it, and I have some questions for you! First of all, what's with the 'I'm nothing but a fading spirit' line you sold me? Because that's looking like a whole load of coal right about now! What about a new fifth Mysticon being called?" She reached out and pushed a finger against the

Rogue's very non-spirity, very solid shoulder as she continued. "What about Doug?"

The Rogue's grin grew wider. "What about Doug?" she retorted. "What about any of you, in fact? Because you see, I just remembered something." She poked Em's shoulder, hard, in return. "You left the door open." She spun on her heel and sprinted up the path, past the ice statues, heading for the first puzzle and, beyond it . . .

"The portal!" Arkayna shouted. "She's going for the portal!"

The five of them raced through the ravine, across the huge triangular canyon, up and up the narrowing path toward the surface. They skidded and slid across the ice, scrambling up to the portal. But there was no one there. They were too late.

The Rogue was free.

In Which an Old Deal

Becomes New News

17

EM TUMBLED THROUGH THE PORTAL INTO THE STRONGHOLD
first, rolling to her feet and holding her shield ready to
protect her friends as they came through behind her.

But there was no sign of the Rogue. She had definitely
been here, though: Malvaron lay dazed on the floor at
Em's feet, and Choko hopped frantically up and down on
his chest, patting his face to revive him.

"Oof!" Arkayna spilled out of the portal behind Em
and crashed into her back.

"Ack!" Zarya followed a split second later.

"Careful, don't step on Malvaron!" Em circled around him, still scanning the edges of the room for threats. Behind her, she heard Piper and Doug stumble through the portal.

"Oh no, Malvaron! Is he all right?" Arkayna asked Choko, kneeling down beside him.

The foz nodded, then shrugged, then resumed patting Malvaron's face. With a splutter, Malvaron suddenly sat up. Choko chirped in alarm as he fell backward onto the ground, then looked up at Arkayna and nodded decisively.

"I'm glad you're okay," Malvaron said to Arkayna, then glanced around at the rest of them. "All of you. I was about to go through the portal to find you, but she surprised me, knocked me down, and ran off." He rubbed his head ruefully. "I never saw her coming. I guess it's true what they said about her."

"Wait, what did they say? 'They' who?" Arkayna leaned forward eagerly. "What did you find?"

"After you left, I did more research into that particular portal spell," Malvaron explained. "I found it deep in

Astromancer lore. It's not part of a curse at all. That girl was . . . well, she wasn't—"

"Yeah, we know this part," Piper interrupted. "The fifth Mysticon is a baddie."

Malvaron shook his head, then winced at the motion. "No, that's just it. She's not the fifth Mysticon. She's not a Mysticon at all."

Across the room, Em's shoulders sagged. "Oh no," she murmured. She dismissed her shield and dropped down heavily on the couch.

"She fought alongside the Mysticons for a while, as if she was part of the team," Malvaron continued. "Her name was Adakite Flowstone, but she called herself 'Mysticon Rogue.'" He shrugged. "I feel like they should have known something was up when she picked that name, you know? But she had known the original Dragon Mage a long time—they were friends from before the original Mysticons were called—so I guess they trusted her. Plus, she was a great tactician and a naturally gifted magician. She shaped—shapes—her magic to look like Mysticon magic, but none of her powers come from the Codex."

"So what went wrong?" Zarya asked. "Sounds like she'd have been useful to have on your side, as long as she kept her attitude in check."

"You got it in one," said Malvaron. "She couldn't. She wanted to be famous like the Mysticons, but she didn't want to be part of the team. She wanted to be the star, the *most* loved, the *most* feared. Plus, the Astromancers didn't treat her like a Mysticon, which made her mad. And the people of the city didn't adore her like they did the rest of the team, which made her madder. So pretty quickly, she gave up on being the most loved and focused on being the most feared. She went where she thought she could get more power. She went to Necrafa."

"She betrayed her friends to *Necrafa*?" cried Arkayna. "That's awful!"

"Sounds like she didn't do it all at once," Malvaron replied. "From what the Astromancers could tell, pretty soon after the Mysticons were called, Necrafa made the Rogue a secret offer in exchange for spying on the team. The Rogue started feeding Necrafa bits of information—never enough to seriously hurt the Mysticons, but just enough to keep Necrafa on the hook for more."

"Playing both sides," Zarya muttered.

"She is a sneaky sneak!" Piper decided. "Who sneaks!"

"Or maybe she was conflicted," said Malvaron. "Who knows? In any case, it didn't last. Imani Firewing noticed how her former friend was changing. She found evidence that Adakite was about to join Necrafa for good and confronted her. Adakite panicked and tried to run, but the Mysticons and Astromancers were ready. They knew the Rogue was too dangerous for any regular prison. So they set up the Chillwaste just for her."

"We have to find her!" Arkayna said. She stood and pulled Malvaron to his feet as well. "Was there anything in the Astromancer lore about where she might go?"

"Ooh!" Em said, rummaging in her pouch, desperate to be helpful. "I have a Seeker Orb in here somewhere. Would that work?"

"The Rogue is very, very good at hiding," replied Malvaron gloomily. "She's not going to be found if—"

"Uh, hey." Doug had wandered over to the TV during the discussion and now was peering at it intently. "I think I found her."

Everyone crowded around to look. A news bulletin

was playing on the floating screen, showing an image of the Astromancer Academy, looking across the water from the city proper. Necrafa and her spectres were arrayed in the skies above the Academy. As Em ducked around Doug's arm to get a better view, Necrafa directed a squad of spectres to swoop down on the Academy's dome. The Astromancers, levitating just above the dome, drove the spectres back. Runes pulsed in the air, forming shields that repelled the winged skeletons.

Choko squeaked angrily, pointing to the bottom of the screen.

"I see her!" Em said.

"Not . . . not that sneaky, actually," mused Piper.

A black-and-gold blur streaked from the city toward the Academy. Malvaron gestured, and as the volume on the TV went up they heard Serena's excited voice. The gorgon reporter was demanding, "Are you getting this?" and, dimly, Em could hear the snakes that made up her hair repeating, *"Are you getting thisssss?"* Then Serena composed herself, clearing her throat. "Ahem. It appears someone else is entering the fray. You heard it here first; there is a new development in today's Academy attack.

And whoever it is appears to be running on water! But the real question, loyal viewers, is this: Whose side are they on? As soon as we know the answer, you will, too!"

Em's heart sank. She knew the answer. The Rogue was finally going to join Necrafa.

In Which There Is Stress,
a Song, and a Scheme

18

EM PACED BACK AND FORTH IN FRONT OF THE TV. "THIS IS ALL my fault!" she said. "I knew there was something off about her from the minute she started talking to me. I should have trusted my instincts. I should have paid closer attention to what the puzzles were trying to tell us. I should have thought it all through. I should never have been so quick to believe any of it—the convenient curse, her conveniently fading spirit, Doug conveniently becoming a Mysticon. . . ." She stopped and looked up at Doug. "Not that I don't think . . . Doug, I didn't mean that you aren't . . . I'm sorry!"

Doug shook his head and sat down heavily. "No, you're right. It was great having an adventure with you—scary, but great. But I know I'm no hero."

"Hey, no, that's not what I'm saying *at all*!" said Em, rushing over to him. She couldn't stand that she had made him doubt himself. Reaching out and patting his knee awkwardly, she went on: "I told you before we ever heard of a fifth Mysticon: You *are* a hero."

"We couldn't have made it through the Chillwaste without you," Arkayna said.

"That's just a fact," Zarya added. "You were amazing against the rocs."

"You kept us together when we would have split up," said Em.

"Aaaaaaand," Piper said, pointing at the blackened toy still held in Doug's hands, "you sacrificed your poor pega-corn. If that's not heroic, I don't know what is."

Doug's eye welled up with tears. "Thanks, guys, that means a lot. I just . . . I thought I was going to be able to do more. To be more. I want to help you fight the Rogue

and Necrafa, but I'm no Mysticon. I don't have any powers. I'm just me. I don't know what to do."

"Aw, don't cry, big guy." Piper threw her arms around
his neck. "We'll figure it out! Remember what Gnomez 2
Men always say: 'It's Not So Bad'!" She struck a pose and
started to sing.

> *"You have to fight a titan but it's*
> *three dwarves in a coat,*
> *You're scared to sing your solo but*
> *you never miss a note,*
> *You're naked in the classroom but*
> *turns out it's just a dream,*
> *Oh baby, things really aren't as bad*
> *as they seem!"*

She held her arms out to Em. "Come on, do the next
chorus with me!"

Em chuckled. "Piper, I'm not sure now is the time. . . ."

Piper shot Em a pointed look. "Now is the *perfect* time.
Our *teammate* needs cheering up. Riiiiiight?"

Em glanced over at Doug and saw him looking back

at her with a glimmer of hope in his eye, the anxiety in his face just starting to fade. She would do anything to make him feel sure of himself again. Even this. She threw one hand in the air, cocked her hip to the side, and sang, *"So when you're feeling overwhelmed, like you don't have a chance . . ."*

Choko began cheeping and drumming his paws to the beat as Piper ran up next to Em, and together they continued:

> *"Girl, throw your hands up, do a twirl*
> *and go into your dance!*
> *Remember that it's darkest just before*
> *the sunlight gleams,*
> *Oh baby, it's really not as bad as*
> *it seems!*
> *Ooh-hoo, girl, it's really not as bad*
> *as it seems!"*

The three of them flung their hands out toward Doug in a final pose, grinning broadly. Doug couldn't help himself; he burst into applause while Arkayna, Zarya, and

Malvaron laughed. The tension in the room was broken for a moment.

Em took a deep breath. "What I was trying to say is, you mean a lot to us, to this team, even if you don't have powers. Even when you don't know what to do."

Arkayna came up behind Em and put her hands on Em's shoulders. "She's right." She looked down at Em. "And that goes for you, too, you know."

"What?" Em blushed. She didn't even know why she was blushing; it just happened.

Arkayna turned Em around to face her. "You blame yourself for the Rogue getting out. You blame yourself for a *lot*, but you just wanted to help. You want everyone to feel important and included, even thousand-year-old cranky spirits. And that's amazing. But don't forget, you're important, too. Even when you don't know what to do."

"I . . . I know." Em couldn't stop blushing. Why couldn't she stop blushing? *Stop it, face*, she thought. It didn't help. She forced herself to meet Arkayna's eyes and grinned at her ruefully. She *did* know. Most of the time.

Then they heard Doug muttering, almost to himself. He was still smiling a little, and he looked resigned rather than upset as he said, "Man, I really don't know why I got my hopes up there. How could I ever be like her? I mean, she's so fast, and small, and . . . fast! I'm not like that at all."

Arkayna gasped. "He's right! That's it! *None* of us are like that!"

Piper shrugged. "I don't know. I'm pretty fast."

"No," Arkayna said, "I mean, that's why Adakite needed us to come unlock the puzzles for her—because we have what she doesn't. The solutions to those locks were all about selflessness and teamwork, which she obviously doesn't understand. *That's* how the original Mysticons trapped her. And *that's* how we beat her."

"Okay, that sounds nice and all, but I'm not hearing a solid plan," Zarya said. "We use teamwork all the time. How is this special?"

"I get it," said Malvaron, nodding in excitement. "She can see a normal trap a mile away. But if she doesn't understand how you think, she won't even know it's coming."

"Yes!" The light dawned on Em. "Adakite bragged to us about all her strengths, and the puzzles showed us all her weaknesses. We *know* this girl, and she doesn't know us; she didn't care about knowing us *at all*. We can get her! All we need is—"

"Bait," Doug finished, perking up. "You need bait. You need me."

In Which the Real Boss Fight Begins

19

ABOVE THE BEATING OF GRIFFIN WINGS, THE RUSH OF THE wind, and the racing of her own heart, Em heard Zarya shout, "Doug, last chance! Are you sure?"

Sitting behind Em on Topaz, Doug nodded once, fiercely. "I can do this!" His hands tightened on Em's shoulders.

She turned to look over her shoulder at him. He had ditched the backpack, but the potion belt, with its remaining two vials, was still slung over his shoulder. He was nervous, but he seemed ready. She squeezed his hand. "You really can, you know," she told him. Then she turned to face the battle in front of them.

The Mysticons and Doug were over halfway to the Astromancer Academy, flying on their griffins just above the surface of the sea. Every second, they got closer and had a better view of how easily Adakite was turning the tide in Necrafa's favor.

While Necrafa and her spectres flew above, waiting and watching intently for the moment, the Rogue wove across the rooftops of the Academy. She leaped off the central dome, disappearing behind one of the surrounding wings, then appeared suddenly in a new position to attack one of the levitating Astromancers from behind. When that Astromancer fell unconscious, the spell he was in charge of flared and sputtered out, leaving a hole in the protective wards that the other magicians scrambled to cover.

But the Academy's defensive line was getting dangerously thin. Adakite had already knocked out half a dozen Astromancers, and a few more were landing on the dome to attend to their fallen friends. Others had clearly been redeployed to deal with the Rogue directly. Clustered in a small group, they fired spells at Adakite and set traps in her path. But she dodged them all.

Soon Em was close enough to see that, just before the Rogue evaded an attack, her headpiece and her eyes flashed gold.

Em steered Topaz closer to Arkayna's griffin, Izzie, where Arkayna was in touch with Malvaron via her bangle-phone. She leaned over to shout at the bangle, "What's with her light show? Can you see that?"

"Yeah, that's True Sight, her most powerful spell," Malvaron responded. "It lets her see through illusions and other magic, and it also enhances all her senses. So assume she can hear everything you say, starting"—Em looked up to see the Rogue's head turn toward them—"right about now."

Em and Arkayna exchanged a glance, and then Arkayna turned to look at Zarya and Piper, flying on her other side. "Did you girls get all that?"

"Loud and clear," said Zarya.

"Mmm-hmm!" Piper nodded emphatically, eyes wide and lips pressed closed.

"Then let's get to work," Arkayna said. She pointed at Doug and smiled. "Step one: naked in the classroom."

"Wha—oh, *right!*" Doug grinned back at Arkayna. Then, in a low whisper to Em, he said, "Man, I wish I could wink right now!"

Breaking formation, Em steered Topaz down to a stony outcropping near the Academy. As Doug clambered off the griffin's back, Em said, "Make sure you stay safe, all right?" She raised her voice as Topaz flew her toward the fight. "Without you and that invincibility potion, our whole plan fails!"

Necrafa raised her head and caught sight of the Mysticons, formed up and charging directly at her. "Children," she hissed. "I have no time for you today." She pointed in their direction and commanded, "Destroy them, my undead spectres! And be quick!"

The spectres abandoned their positions around the Academy and darted toward the griffins.

"Wait . . ." murmured Arkayna as the winged skeletons got closer. "Waaaaait. . . . Now! Three dwarves in a coat!"

Quickly, Zarya, Piper, and Em steered their griffins into a tight triangular formation around Arkayna.

Arkayna held up her staff and summoned a spherical shield, which snapped into place around them a split second before the first of the spectres crashed into it. One after another, the skeletons collided with the barrier, snapping and snarling. Holding their tight formation, the Mysticons lured the spectres up and away from the Astromancers.

Necrafa shrieked in irritation. But she wasn't looking at her ineffective army, she was looking at the Rogue. With the spectres gone, the Astromancers were rallying and strengthening their wards, and Adakite had abandoned her strategy of flanking them from behind. Instead, she was working her way around to the near side of the building.

"Your work is not done!" Necrafa screamed at the Rogue. "You promised me you would *completely* dismantle their defenses!"

"Change of plans," the Rogue sneered. She vaulted between two wings of the building to bring herself lower and lower, then pushed off the stone foundation and began sprinting across the water. She was heading right for Doug!

In Which One Villain Retreats
and Another Comes Too Close

20

THE MYSTICONS ARCED AROUND AND HEADED BACK TOWARD
Necrafa, trailing the army of spectres behind them. From
her position inside the shield, Em saw the Rogue leaping
from the tower. "Arkayna, is it darkest yet?" she asked.

"Not yet," said Arkayna. "We're almost there." She
patted Izzie and called to the griffins, "Fast as you can,
now!"

Flying in perfect formation in their energy sphere, the
Mysticons swooped down on Necrafa. The lich roared in

anger, and waves of red energy poured out of her mouth at them.

Arkayna cried out as the shield dissolved under the onslaught, but it had done its job: The girls and their griffins were unharmed. The Mysticons descended on Necrafa . . . and swept right past her.

While Necrafa wheeled around in confusion, Arkayna shouted, *"Now* it's darkest!" As one, the griffins turned in a tight, perfect arc to face Necrafa and, behind her, the ragged cone of spectres. The skeleton army backwinged frantically to avoid crashing into their mistress and one another.

Arkayna thrust her right arm forward. "Time for some sunlight!" And in the same breath, all four Mysticons unleashed the power of their bracers. *"Release the Dragon!"* commanded Arkayna.

"Fly, Phoenix, fly!" Piper hooted.

"Time to howl!" hollered Zarya.

"Battle Unicorn, charge!" Em shouted as all four bracers glowed brightly. The green Dragon, gold Phoenix, blue Wolf, and magenta Unicorn stormed through the air, knocking Necrafa back and overwhelming the spectres.

Necrafa looked over the chaotic remains of her army, then down at the Rogue, single-mindedly running for Doug. Howling over her shoulder, "I am not done with you yet, Mysticons!" Necrafa retreated into the night.

But there was no time to celebrate. "Doug!" Em yelled at the top of her lungs. "You need to mix that potion *now*!"

Stranded on his rock, surrounded by the sea, Doug fumbled with the belt. He pulled out the last two potions, one bright purple and one a churning red, and popped the tops off the vials.

The Rogue was too fast. She seemed to blink across the water and was suddenly at Doug's side, snatching the vials from his hands. Darting a few steps away, all the distance the jagged outcropping would allow, she glared at Doug. Her eyes glowed gold as she scanned for illusions and traps. Finding none, she snickered in disbelief. "Where is your team now?" she asked Doug slyly. "They left you all alone."

In Which Magic Fails
and a Hug Succeeds

21

"TO THINK, THE MYSTICONS TRUSTED THEIR MOST POWERFUL weapon to *you*," the Rogue laughed, tipping the purple potion into the red one. "In a moment, I will be unstoppable, and you will still be nothing. I can't believe you thought you could be like me!"

She swirled the two liquids together, and *POOF!* The mixture exploded into a thick gray cloud.

"Naw," Doug replied as the Rogue coughed and waved her hands frantically, trying to clear the air. "This time I thought *you* could be like *me*."

The gray haze thinned a bit, revealing Adakite, wearing only a tattered shirt and pants. Her daggers, headpiece, and Rogue outfit were nowhere to be seen. She looked down at herself and gasped, then gestured haughtily, summoning her clothing to return.

Nothing happened. Growling, she tried again.

Still nothing. Beginning to panic, she turned to face the sea and braced herself as if to race away.

"Uh, I wouldn't," said Doug, raising a cautionary finger. "Unless you can run on water without your magic."

"Without my—" she sputtered. "What did you do to me?"

"I didn't do anything." Doug shrugged and gestured at the cloud all around them. "But *you* made an anti-magic potion. That exploded."

Adakite screamed in frustration, then turned to look over the water again. "I can still swim, you know!"

"Try it," said Em, swooping down on Topaz to hover a little distance away, outside the cloud.

"No, really, try it!" Piper urged as Miss Paisley flapped down on the other side of the mist. "It'll be funny!"

"Or you could just stay right there, where I can keep an eye on you," said Zarya, aiming an arrow at her from Archer's back high above. She tilted her head toward Arkayna and Izzie, flying next to her. "Arkayna, you ready to send this girl to her room?"

"You know it," Arkayna said. She raised her staff and began to draw runes in the air.

"Wait a moment," said Adakite, beginning to smile. "You can't fool me again. I'm helpless in here, but *you're* stuck out *there*! You can't come any closer without this mist affecting you too, and neither can your spells"—she looked up at Zarya—"or your arrows. You are all useless without your magic. I haven't lost yet." She turned to Doug. "You. You can get me out of this. Help me escape, and I'll teach you all the magic I know. I'll make you powerful!"

Doug looked at the Mysticons, hovering out of reach all around him.

"Don't look at them!" Adakite stepped toward him. "You'll never be one of them. Join me instead, and I'll make you *matter*!"

Still holding Em's gaze, Doug replied, "No thanks." He turned back to Adakite. "I already matter." He reached out and wrapped her in a huge bear hug, pinning her arms to her sides. She struggled, but he was too strong.

Em broke into a huge grin as all four griffins, right on cue, began beating their wings hard, dispersing the anti-magic haze. As the last of the mist disappeared, Arkayna began to recite:

> *"Attend to my summons, attend*
> *to my knocks,*
> *Keep this girl locked in compassionate*
> *locks,*
> *Take her to faraway ice with*
> *all haste,*
> *Make her a prisoner of the*
> *Chillwaste!"*

The green runes she had traced in the air began to twist around one another, faster and faster, until they formed a glowing ring of crackling energy. The ring fell from the sky, contracting and descending over Adakite's head and shoulders. It spun down through the circle of Doug's arms until it fizzled against the ground, and where it passed over Adakite it seemed to swallow her whole. The Rogue was gone, trapped in the stars once more.

In Which the Day Is Saved,
the Battle Rehashed, a Hope Fulfilled,
and a Hope Deferred

22

THE MYSTICONS AND DOUG JOINED NOVA TERRON AND THE other Astromancers on the roof of the Academy and helped to move the injured magicians safely inside.

As they worked, Nova raised his eyebrows at Arkayna. "I cannot fault your results," said the Star Master, "but your battlefield discussion was . . . interesting. Did I hear you yell something about dwarves in a coat?"

Arkayna laughed. "We knew that the Rogue would hear everything we said, once we got close enough. So we had to use a code."

"We were worried about how powerful she and Necrafa could be together," Zarya added, "but then we realized how easy it would be to split them up. Adakite likes to be the star, after all."

"And we knew she'd *never* be able to resist something as shiny-sounding as an invincibility potion," said Piper, "so we made sure to talk about that *extra*-loud."

"Yeah, we figured if we had something that meant she didn't need Necrafa," Em said, "all we had to do was make that thing seem really easy to get."

Doug chuckled. "That's why I got to be the bait. I don't have any flashy powers, so she'd never see me as a threat."

Nova Terron shook his head. "I remember a thousand years ago, when the Mysticons worked with Star Master Alpha Galaga to design the Chillwaste. It was meant to be more than a prison; it was intended as a lesson. Their hope was that Adakite Flowstone would learn from its puzzles and, in learning, win enough freedom to call to the Mysticons for their forgiveness. Imani Firewing's fondest hope was that, one day, her old friend could rejoin the Mysticons as a trusted ally." He sighed. "That hope seems to have failed."

"Nah, I'm with Imani; there's always hope," said Em.

The others looked at her in surprise, and Piper giggled. "Well, if we *have* to go back there to check on her, I need to teach you all to ice-skate."

Em slung an arm around Piper's shoulders. "Let's worry about that tomorrow," she said, yawning.

"Okay," Piper replied. "Hey, I can't wait to tell Malvaron all about this! How Adakite was like, 'Ooh, I'm so evil, join me!' and Doug was like, 'Never! I am the strongest!' and then Adakite was all, 'Curses!' and then . . .'"

The five of them mounted the griffins and headed for the Stronghold, tired and elated and all talking at once. As they flew, Em watched Doug, bantering and joking right along with the rest of them. He wasn't hesitant or awkward or unsure. He was perfectly comfortable, perfectly included.

And so, Em realized, was she.

"Hey, Em, you there?" Zarya snapped her fingers, and Em registered with a start that she had missed something.

Zarya sighed, smiled, and repeated her question: "I said, do you really think Adakite will learn anything? She seemed pretty stubborn."

Em shrugged. This had been a good day, and she was feeling generous. "You never know," she said. "Maybe in another thousand years?"

ABOUT THE AUTHOR

Liz Marsham began her storytelling career as an editor for DC Comics and Disney Publishing. She lives in Los Angeles with her husband, a cat who thinks she is a princess, and a cat who thinks he is a dog. Visit her (and the cats) at lizmarsham.com.